A Dash of Murder

Pecan Bayou, Volume 1

Teresa Trent

Published by Teresa Trent, 2011.

This is a work of fiction. Similarities to real people, places, or events are entirely coincidental.

A DASH OF MURDER

First edition. September 14, 2011.

Copyright © 2011 Teresa Trent.

ISBN: 978-0984041718

Written by Teresa Trent.

To all the "Dannys" out there, especially my Andrew

CHAPTER ONE

ONE NEED NOT BE A CHAMBER to be haunted;
  One need not be a house;
  The brain has corridors surpassing
  Material place.
  —Emily Dickinson

I looked up at the window of the crumbling, abandoned hospital, and for just a second, I saw it. Filmy and fleeting, it seemed to find me in the midst of the suffocating heat.

"Mom, hurry up. We just need to identify any fungi or lichens, and then I have enough information for my merit badge." My seven-year-old son, Zach, turned his back on me as he waded through the overgrown field of weeds climbing nearly to his blue-jean-clad waist.

The back of my neck prickled even though I was sweating in the afternoon heat. Late October may designate fall in many parts of the country, but in South Texas, it's still summer. My eyes scanned the second story of the dilapidated building and I felt a strangely unwelcome chill. Was someone up there? The gray windows with mismatched glass shards resembled razor-sharp teeth. At second glance, they seemed empty now.

We were standing in front of the Johnson Tuberculosis Hospital, empty and shuttered for the last forty years. So many souls had passed through here – it felt as if a part of them lingered. The hospital opened in the 1920s, providing therapy and rest from the ills of tuberculosis. Now the faded brick and shattered windows were merely a lonely reminder of its importance long ago.

"Betsy!"

At the sound of my name, I looked around to see Danny, my twenty-four-year-old cousin with Down syndrome, running across the front lawn of the hospital, the weeds swishing at his ankles. He held a Scout book, the pages now flapping at his side.

"Betsy," Danny said, "at the job, my friend Ellie said it's cold where her grandma is. Why isn't it cold here? Why, Betsy?"

Danny's "job" was doing general clean-up work at our local fast food restaurant. I picked him up from work today to help out my Aunt Maggie. A pleasant aroma of French fries was still about him.

"Because we live in Texas, and Ellie's grandma lives up north somewhere."

I turned around to see Zach standing dangerously close to a plant with three leaves, which meant either poison ivy or poison oak. When my only child decided to work on his plant science merit badge for his Texas Scout Achievement, he could have chosen the required 100' x 100' plot of land anywhere. I don't know why we had to look at weeds in front of this falling-down, ancient building.

This property had been neglected for years, and was now overgrown by prickle poppies, buffalo burrs, pigweed and devil's horn. I slapped at a mosquito. The temperature was in the 90s, as it had been for the last three months, and it seemed the heat and humidity would never end. We were just a few days from Halloween and still sweating.

"Ooh, Mom. I just found a broomweed." Zach pointed to a yellow flower in a patch of weeds.

"Good, the witches can use that on Halloween," I said.

Danny laughed. "There is no such thing as witches, Betsy. No witches, no monsters and no ghosts!"

I nodded in agreement, and pulled at my blouse to unstick it from my body. Again, I caught movement out of the corner of my eye. I focused back up at the window of the old hospital. Were we not alone? Was someone walking around in there?

"Zach, do you see anybody up in that window?"

Zach looked up, squinting his brown eyes in the ray of sun aimed at us. I waited as he scanned each window in the crumbling building. A bird squawked behind us, piercing the quiet. Zach looked back at me with a scowl. "No." He returned to his clipboard.

Danny put his hands together around his mouth and shouted at the empty building. "Hello? Hello? Anybody home?"

I blew out an exasperated sigh. "Okay. Must be the heat."

I have to admit, I stayed indoors as much as possible during the summer months, especially when it felt like this. Why go out and sweat when I could be inside with the air conditioning humming and the computer glowing?

My Aunt Maggie would say the thing in the window was an apparition of some type, or a residual haunting of someone who lived or worked at the hospital. Ghost hunting had become one of her hobbies after my uncle Jeeter died. She was a card-carrying member of the Pecan Bayou Paranormal Society, which consisted of Maggie, Howard Gunther and Birdie Bryant.

Birdie was a snowbird and would probably show up around Thanksgiving and stay in Pecan Bayou until Memorial Day. It was too bad she wouldn't be around for the upcoming Halloween weekend. Maggie and Howard sorely needed her for the biggest project their group had ever tackled. I especially would have liked to see her, as I was the one who was volunteered to take her place.

"Mom?"

I turned from the building to see Zach, who was holding his clipboard to his chest. He looked up at me, eyebrow raised.

"What are you looking at?"

"I don't know. I thought I saw something."

"Like what?" He was beginning to pick up on my anxiety. I was being silly, and I knew my slight discomfort could turn into a giant fear in Zach. I needed to lighten the mood. A smile spread across my face, reassuring him all was well.

"Like ... ghosts!" I wailed and chased him and Danny around the patch of spindly greenery. They both giggled and shrieked as they ran through the tall weeds and flying insects. The sound seemed to echo against the aging bricks and decaying structure. Zach ran with wild abandon and hoisted himself up to a three-foot-high brick wall that had served as an enclosure for a courtyard.

"You can't get me!" he taunted, standing on the top of the wall.

"Zach, you better get down from there!" Danny yelled from the other side of the field. "You'll break your ..."

Zach twisted his little body around to see his cousin. It was then that he fell backwards onto the concrete courtyard behind the wall, and I heard a sickening, snapping sound.

IN THE DOCTOR'S OFFICE, Zach sat holding his arm and rocking while Danny sat next to him repeating, "It's going to be okay. It's going to be okay."

I stood at a frosted glass window in the reception area, feeling ridiculous tapping at it for the third time. The receptionist slid the dividing window back. She was wearing blue scrubs with white butterflies on them.

"Have you heard anything from Dr. MacPhee yet?" I asked, while glancing over my shoulder at Zach, still rocking in pain.

"Yes, Mrs. Livingston. He is on his way." Her smile was tight, and her dark brown hair was coiled at the back of her head. Not a hair would dare fall out of place. She put her red lacquered fingernails back on the glass door and slid it shut with a resounding click.

"It hurts, Mom," Zach whimpered.

"I know, baby, I know. Dr. Mac will be here in just a moment." I sat back down next to Zach and started to put my arm around him, but then thought better of it.

"It's going to be okay," Danny repeated.

"Will I have to have a shot?" Zach asked, a tear settling at the rim of his eyelid. It wouldn't take much to push it down his dirt-streaked face.

"I don't know," I answered honestly. "But you might get a cast for everyone to sign."

"Really?"

"Cool," Danny said.

The door to the street opened, letting in rushes of hot air. Dr. Mac, flushed from the heat, came directly over to us. He was in his late sixties with silver-gray hair and a rather round middle. With a beard, he could double as Santa Claus and would probably be asked to play him at the hospital Christmas party in a couple of months. He dropped his car key into his pocket, and I heard it jangle against some change.

"Zachary Livingston, what happened? Have you been living life on the wild side again?" He smiled as he bent down and tenderly touched Zach's arm. Dr. Mac's eyes never left the broken bone.

"I'm so sorry it took me some time to get here. Mrs. MacPhee has me running all over town. Our daughter, Ellen is getting married right before Thanksgiving, and she is entertaining the future in-laws tonight. I was out picking up table linens for her. As a matter of fact, I'll put a cast on Zachary and then I have to be out the door again."

"Thank you so much for making time for us. We could have gone to the emergency room, but I just thought it would be a lot easier with you working on him."

"Don't you think a thing about it. For Zachary here, I will gladly interrupt my honey-do list."

I sighed in relief, feeling grateful for the many days like today. Mac was the doctor who had delivered Zach and helped me through that awful time when I had felt so alone. That was when he asked me to call him Mac instead of Dr. MacPhee.

He told me that if we were going to be spending all this time together we should at least be on a first-name basis. Thanks to him and people like him, that part of my life was just a bad dream now. It was hard to believe so much time had passed since then. When we started this doctor/patient relationship, I was married, pregnant and about to be conned.

CHAPTER TWO

SEVEN YEARS EARLIER

I stretched out my arms to my husband as he walked up the broken concrete we called a sidewalk.

Barry came through the squeaky screen door of the rental house. "I'm home," he said, the tiredness creeping into his voice. His greeting was followed by a hacking cough that sounded deep in his chest. I was hoping he felt better tonight.

Barry had been expecting me to rush out the door to my own job at the Alamo Grand Theater, but instead I had squeezed my balloon-shaped body into a black sleeveless dress. Hoping he wouldn't notice how little room there was in the dress, I flounced my long brown hair to give it fullness. I had seen this in a movie while I had been walking up and down the aisles looking for people with their feet on the seats. I even practiced it in the mirror earlier that day. I leaned against the doorway of our tiny kitchen and put on my best Marlena Dietrich voice.

"Hello." Sexiness was practically oozing out of my vocal cords.

Barry loosened the tie on his white shirt and smiled. His light blue eyes crinkled at the corners. "Well ... hello. Listen,

I don't know who you are, but I'll bet my wife will be back any moment." He sighed, and I walked over, taking him into my arms. He pulled back slightly, his eyes taking in my ever-so-seductive outfit.

"That dress just barely fits you. I wonder if it will even fit after the baby's here."

He was right. It was too tight, but so was our budget. He lowered his lips onto mine and kissed me. Maestro, cue the violins. A warmth spread through me. We were finding the same old wonderful us. I reveled in the moment, and then he pulled his face back and looked at me, not moving, not progressing.

"Barry?"

"Yes?" His eyes drifted towards the closed closet door to the left of me. I chose to ignore it. We were on our way to being fine, and I wasn't stopping.

"Barry, I don't have to go to the theater tonight."

His crystal-blue eyes pulled back to mine. "Um, yes I gathered that."

"I thought that maybe we could ..."

His face took on a scowl as he shook his head. "Are you sure that's a good idea? I mean with all that the doctor said."

The violins in my romantic fantasy came to a screeching halt.

"The doctor said that there was a chance of a disability. These tests aren't foolproof, you know."

"I know. A chance of a disability."

I reached up and pushed a stray hair out of his face. He must have left his suit jacket in the car again. When he was showing property, he always dressed in a full suit no matter how hot the weather.

Barry's partner was the same way. Barry had been a part of Canfield Investments for almost two years now. In that time, he had brought home exactly four commission checks. It was a wonder how we made the money stretch. Once the baby arrived, I knew money would be extremely tight.

"So?" My voice led upward.

"So, well ... I can't stop thinking about Danny. Your aunt and uncle had to give up their lives to take care of him. If something like that should happen ... well, I'm just not sure I'm up for it."

"They wouldn't say they've given up their lives. If anything, they would say he made their lives better, richer and happier. Besides that, it's not going to happen." His grip tightened on my arms as if he were fighting off a wave of aggravation.

My own anger began to rise in my throat. "And what good does it do to go there, Barry? Why are we stressing out about a situation that may never happen to us? Why?"

He let go of me and backed up, yanking at his unfastened tie. "I don't know. You're probably right."

He gazed at the floor and then back up at me, seeming to gain control of his emotions. His voice was strained but tender. "Listen, why don't you take this evening to get off your feet and rest, and keep that baby healthy? I ran out of cough drops at work, and I won't sleep tonight if I can't get this hacking to stop. I'll be right back, okay?"

Even though it wasn't the evening I wanted, he did, at least, seem to be trying to find some peace with his fears. Worrying about something that may or may not happen could make anybody crazy. Maybe we could get back on track and restart this evening, just not in the way I had planned.

"Okay. I guess I'll put our romantic evening on hold."

He took my hand in his. I loved the feeling of his hand surrounding mine. "Good. I hope you can understand I don't want to take any chances with our baby. I'm trying to believe everything will be okay, but I have to at least know I did all I could to ensure the baby's safety." He looked at the feast I had prepared for our anniversary dinner. "Oh, and I already ate. You should probably go ahead and eat."

He kissed me on the forehead, lingering just a little too long, and with that, Barry was out the door and on his way.

I kicked off my black heels, blew out the candles I'd lit and started putting the dinner into plastic containers. Barry was always right about things concerning me. He had big dreams of success in his world of investing. He told me how he planned to start here in Pecan Bayou, then as the company grew, we would move to Dallas or Houston where he and Canfield would have offices. We would be a part of a country club and associate with the wealthiest people in the state. It seemed he was training to be a somebody, and I loved that about him. I was more of a tomboy than the Junior League material he had no doubt envisioned, but he was always there to guide me, and I was thankful.

I changed out of my stretched-out little black dress and into my pink cotton maternity gown, then stretched out on the couch to wait for Barry. That was just the beginning of a long, long wait.

It wasn't until later I found out he had a bag already packed in the trunk of his car. In the closet, he had stowed another bag and his golf clubs. I would have loved to wrap at least one of those clubs around his neck. I guess he was planning to slip out while I was at work. No divorce, no child support, no shared custody. Life's too hard – see you later. His plan would have worked perfectly if I hadn't planned my little surprise. How did I not see this coming? Fairytale endings may happen to other women, but not to me. Somehow, I had failed.

CHAPTER THREE

JUST LIKE THE BABY growing inside me, I also grew in ways I couldn't imagine. Once my life began AB – After Barry – I realized that maybe I had settled in life. When Barry first left, I felt like someone had just pushed the handle and was happily flushing me down the drain. Instead of feeling pregnant, I felt fat and undesirable.

Barry had constantly pointed out I didn't dress right. I didn't have that casual chic look that would be appropriate for his future life. He wanted a wife with that look of natural beauty that only money could buy.

I always felt uncomfortable out on business dinners with Barry, his partner and various clients. If he felt I had made some sort of social blunder, you could bet he would certainly replay the entire conversation from the evening when we returned home.

My hair is chestnut brown and shoulder-length now, but back then at his request, I had dyed my hair blonde. He thought blonde women were sexier, somehow. The fact is, the world is full of blonde women who aren't sexy, and for a short while, I was one of them.

Nothing I did, nothing I said, nothing at all seemed to be up to Barry's standards. When the prenatal test predicted we might not have a picture-perfect baby on the way, the news was just too much for him. I had fallen short. I was not worthy. He had at first been worried the baby wouldn't be a boy, so the idea of a disability was earth-shattering for him.

After my husband left, I found out he hadn't been too adept at facing the truth in other ways as well. I discovered a shoebox full of bills hidden on the top shelf of his closet. We were young, and I was dumb, believing that four lousy commission checks paid enough salary to support us with a home and fairly new car, which he took with him. He was kind enough to leave me with his old clunker, a Chevy station wagon. Not only were we behind on bills for prenatal care at the doctor's office, but Barry had made some terrible investments at the advice of his partner, Canfield. Our finances were a ticking time bomb, which exploded the week after he left. The bank started calling me about repossessing the car. The mortgage company wanted to know when I planned to catch up on three outstanding payments. I was deep in debt, and all I had was a lousy job at the movie theater to pay it all off. Barry didn't even resemble the man I thought he was.

When Zach arrived, I faced raising him as a single parent. I had not planned to share too much about Barry with Zach. It just seemed cruel, and the kids at school would probably take care of that for me. Nevertheless, Zach grew up harboring some fantasy that his dad was lost or hurt but would show up as a hero, just like the last page of a superhero graphic novel.

A month after Barry's exit, I went to my first Lamaze class with my Aunt Maggie instead of my husband. It was then I began to feel stirrings – not from the baby, although he did pitch in a healthy, happy kick now and again. No, these were stirrings of anger. I went home and grabbed Barry's golf clubs out of the front hall closet where they had sat idle since that eventful night. I lifted the heavy fake leather bag and almost fell back with the counter weight of the baby I was carrying. I lugged the bag and clubs out to the trash can. Barry would have pitched a fit if he had seen me. He would have been sure to tell me just how much those stupid iron sticks cost him. I figured they had cost me a whole lot more. Maybe I didn't want to work in a theater taking tickets for the rest of my life so I could pay off the lifestyle he thought he should have. Maybe I wanted to pursue something that was not in his plans. I wanted to pursue something of my own. I had to find a way to support myself and my child.

I was now going to be a single parent, and working at the theater was not going to support me and my son. I wanted to take control of the chaos I found myself in and needed to come up with my own life plan.

In college, I majored in English. I could easily be a teacher if I went back for my teaching certificate, but the idea of teaching had never appealed to me. I liked to write, but I didn't picture myself a novelist, and I wouldn't be putting out any bodice-rippers with my experiences in that area. So there I was with a degree I didn't know how to use and a pile of bills so large I could repaper the kitchen with them.

One thing about me that seemed useless at the time was my collection. I didn't collect dolls or antiques. I didn't collect first editions or Depression glass. I collected advice. Need to get that nasty ring out of your tub? Need to get lipstick out of your collar? I knew how. It was all in my collection.

I started collecting helpful hints as a young girl, beginning with an old notebook where I painstakingly recorded hundreds of tips in my childhood handwriting. I picked them up from everywhere – old cookbooks, people I knew, hints columns in the newspaper. I suppose my hobby could have stemmed from not having a mother around – a kid trying to have a normal home, even though my dad was a full-time policeman. But whatever the reason, by the time I was twelve I had categorized and alphabetized all the hints I had collected, and had added to it steadily, year after year. Eventually I started recording them on my laptop.

One night after Barry left, as I sat trying not to answer the phone because I was sure there would be a bill collector on the other end, I had an epiphany. What if I turned my household hints into a blog? What if I made my extensive database of knowledge an ongoing source of inspiration for others? I created my blog that night and waited for the hits. Thinking of other ways to make money with my collection, I approached the town paper, The Pecan Bayou Gazette, and the editor agreed to pay me a small amount for a weekly column. He also wanted to include my blog on the Gazette website.

I walked out of the newspaper office that day and gave my waiting Aunt Maggie a hug. I had preferred to go to my interview alone, but I was due any day, and she hovered over me constantly.

"Well Betsy, sunshine or shadows?" Aunt Maggie said. This was a little game we had played since I was a child.

"Sunshine, Aunt Maggie!" She reached out to hug me, and just as I embraced her, I felt a sharp pang in my side. Zachary had decided this would be a fine day to enter the world. Fourteen hours later, Dr. Mac delivered him. From that day on, things got better for me.

Eventually my blog and column following increased, and I found myself making a small income from it. The day a local book publisher called me and asked if I would compile some of my work, I knew we would be okay. I quit the theater the day I received my first book advance. I lined up all my bills in a notebook and created a payment schedule. I paid off one bill and then put those payments toward the balance of another.

The best part about my job as a columnist – by now known as "The Happy Hinter" – was that I was able to do most of my work from the house. Maybe it was just easier to hide out in my house. And, well, there was always the outside chance Barry would return. I would hate to miss him. I now had everything I had before in my life, except a pile of debt and a hyper-critical husband. Yes, sometimes it was a little lonely, but the peace of knowing it was all behind me was immeasurable. I found the idea of dating extremely frightening. I had so misjudged Barry, and I wasn't sure if I knew how to recognize an honest, responsible, kind man. My father was a man like that. But men like my father didn't seem to exist in my generation. So here I was, seven years later, The Happy Hinter, popular blogger, columnist and author. No one needed to know this hinter hadn't always been happy.

TODAY I WAS DRIVING to Benny's Barbecue, a lovely little restaurant about a block off Main Street. Benny was Zach's Scout leader and owner of the restaurant. Benny had read my weekly column in the Pecan Bayou Gazette and asked me to do what he called an "efficiency evaluation" of his business. I hadn't ever considered this kind of thing, but I was more than willing to give it a try. I had done some research and now had a few ideas to present to him. Frankly, for all the time he had spent being a fill-in Scout dad with my son, if Benny had asked for a kidney, I probably would have told him to pick a side.

As I pulled into a slanted parking space in front of the restaurant, I watched Benny as he stood on a ladder, hanging a skeleton in the window with a sign that read, "Yum! I need some BBQ!" The door into the restaurant had a smiling pig painted on it, and pots of bright flowers hung on the front porch of the building. There were also a couple of rocking chairs tourists would sit in during wildflower season, but now they were empty. No one in their right mind would sit outside in this heat.

I mentally rolled through the suggestions I had for Benny. I planned to suggest he switch from plastic cups to glass, which would not only be good for the environment, but Benny's pocketbook as well. He could also soak dirty dishes in tubs of water before washing, to save on hot water costs. I decided to tackle the menu as well to see if Benny could add some side dishes to several meals in order to cut down on food waste.

The bell on the door jangled when I entered, and I smelled the oh-so-pleasant aroma of meat simmering in barbecue sauce. Who could resist this place?

"Hi, Betsy," Benny said, as he wobbled down the ladder. "I really appreciate you coming in this morning."

Benny's restaurant was one of the busiest in town. He juggled running his business with taking care of his wife — with a baby on the way — and two rambunctious boys. His family was also pretty active in the African Methodist Episcopal Church.

"Thanks for giving me the chance to return the favor for all you do for Zach." I took out a clipboard and pen and began to walk around the restaurant. There was plenty of sun streaming in through the side windows, so I made a note that energy could be saved by rolling down the blinds in the afternoon. Looking around, I spied a framed picture near the register. Benny was standing with another man who looked vaguely familiar. They were cutting a red ribbon in front of Benny's restaurant. Where had I seen that guy before?

"Is that the day you opened up?"

Benny was returning to the room after putting away the ladder. "Well, sort of. It's the day we re-opened after some financing. Seems like a long time ago now." He faded off.

As we toured the restaurant, I wrote down a few more ideas. His wife, Celia, came out from the back dressed in jeans and a pink t-shirt with a spotless white apron protecting her clothing. She was holding her back as women who were nine months pregnant were prone to do. She looked tired as she wiped down the already impeccably clean tables.

"Hey, Betsy." She looked pleased to see me, and then her gaze drifted to her husband. "Lunch crowd's due soon," she reminded him.

"Yes," Bennie replied, then turned back to me. "Well, before we get to working here, don't forget to have Zach at the campout around noon on Halloween. Has he found a camper-friendly costume yet?"

"Uh, we're working on it."

"Okay. Just no scary-killer-in-the-woods kind of thing," he added.

"When's the baby due, Celia?" I asked.

She stood up from the table she was cleaning, and stretched. "Soon, I hope. Doctor Green says two more weeks. The way I feel today, it's going to be a long two weeks."

"You can say that again." It was out of Benny's mouth before he could take it back. That was then the rag Celia was holding slapped flat on his head.

"You better watch out. I just may have it sooner if only to get you to be quiet," she said. "Look at me, Betsy. I feel like an elephant. Everything on me has swollen up this time, even my fingers." She held up her hands, showing a line where her wedding ring probably rested up until about a month ago. She had even outgrown that.

Benny grabbed her by the waist and gave her a quick but tender kiss. "I love you no matter what state you're in." It was embarrassing to be standing there seeing two people so obviously in love, and yet it was wonderful.

Pregnancy sure was different for them than it had been for me and Barry.

CHAPTER FOUR

"WATCH OUT, BETSY, SOME of these old floorboards may be treacherous." I followed Aunt Maggie through the rooms full of cracked plaster, floor debris and the ever-present graffiti sprayed on the walls of the former tuberculosis hospital.

Aunt Maggie was a tiny woman at four-foot-eight, and the world often towered above her. Her height was the only part of her that was small. She had the strongest will and the biggest heart in Texas.

"This is going to be great when we film here on Halloween, the scariest night of the year. I'm so glad you could take a few hours away from your tip-writin' column to help us out. The Pecan Bayou Texas Paranormal Society thanks you, and if we find a ghost – boy howdy – I thank you."

"Well, I can spare a few hours here and there."

"So, what are you writin' about now?"

"Um, I'm working on my pre-Thanksgiving columns. Hey, I have a question for you. What would you say is the best way to get red wine out of a tablecloth?"

"You know, Aunt Ida had an unusual way of doing that."

"You mean Aunt Ida, the one who used to bring the chocolate pecan pie when she came for Thanksgiving?" I had not seen great Aunt Ida much since she moved to the retirement center near Austin.

"That's the one. She used to drape her tablecloth over a bowl with the wine stain positioned over the middle of the bowl. Then she would pour salt on the stain, and pour boiling water over the salt, into the bowl. Darndest thing. Took it right out," Maggie said.

For our other-worldly walk-through today, Aunt Maggie dressed for the occasion with a black cap on her head adorned with glow-in-the-dark letters that read "Paranormal Investigator."

She noticed my gaze. "You like it? I ordered one for everyone on the crew, and a few extras. I thought we ought to look official, bein' on TV and all." My aunt's honey-colored bouffant hairdo was all crammed up in the cap with sprayed curls poking out in places.

"Can't wait to wear mine." I was not someone who looked terrific in a ball cap. At least that was what Barry had said. Funny how after all these years I still felt rejected by him.

Maggie stepped around the trash that littered the main hallway. As we came to the end of the passage, her voice lowered slightly. "This up here was what they called the 'dead tunnel.' I saw it in the blueprints Howard had."

Howard was the head of Aunt Maggie's paranormal group. Even though he himself sometimes looked like a person mental health officials might be interested in observing, he was extremely intelligent and had a doctorate in paranormal psychology. I didn't even know a person could get a degree in ghost hunting, but Howard had done it.

Maggie continued her story. "It was the tunnel they used to wheel the bodies to the morgue. That way the live patients wouldn't know about the ones who died. They called it the *dead tunnel.*" I never got too frightened by horror movies, but walking through this part of the hospital certainly gave me a legitimate case of the heebie-jeebies. The dead tunnel was windowless and grimy, and I felt as if we were walking into a mineshaft, not a morgue.

"So here we are." Aunt Maggie's voice took on a softer tone as if we had just entered a funeral home. "Looks a little longer than it did in the blueprints."

We stepped gingerly through the open door where a sign, hanging askew, read, "Hospital Personnel Only: No Visitors Beyond This Point."

Unless you're dead, I thought. Then you are welcome to come on in and sit a spell.

"Aunt Maggie, we can still go get Howard. He's roaming around somewhere here," I said.

"What are we? Chickens? We can do this, Betsy." With that, she shined her heavy-duty flashlight down the tunnel. The tunnel seemed to go on and on, leading into absolute darkness. A million things could be down that hall. My rational fear was that the tunnel would be lined with old furniture or antiquated medical equipment that we would be banging into at any moment. I didn't want to acknowledge my *irrational* fear. Being called a chicken did nothing to raise my confidence and charge me up about venturing down the dead tunnel.

I nodded dully in agreement as my eyes tried to lock onto anything solid in the dark.

"You're making fun of me, I know, but it is true, Betsy. I sense something here. I just hope we can get this on tape when we have a thermal energy camera pointed at it."

According to Howard, a thermal energy camera would capture cold and hot spots that the human eye couldn't see. We stepped forward, our footfalls now echoing against the chilled stone.

As Maggie spoke, I felt a cold breeze hit me. I clenched my bare arms as I felt goose bumps cover my skin. It seemed as if we had phantom air conditioning in this part of the hospital. Down at the end of the blackness I could hear a faint sound — an odd high, chirping, clicking sound. Somehow I hadn't imagined a ghost clicking at me. Maybe there were some tap-dancing spirits floating around.

"It has arrived," Maggie whispered.

"No," I said, trying to squelch the shake that had come into my voice. "A ... draft has arrived, that's all."

"Think what you want, my dear."

She angled the wavering beam of light into the black recesses of the tunnel. From the other end I could hear a distinct rustling sound as something headed our way.

"The apparition is coming near us," Maggie sounded delighted.

"What should we do, Aunt Maggie?" I asked, the volume of my voice rising as the rustling became an increasing cacophony of noise.

Maggie looked down the passage and then yelled, "HOLD YOUR GROUND!"

She stood with her hands placed firmly on her rounded hips, the light of the flashlight now pointed towards the floor.

The wind started blowing her hat off, releasing the strands of hair that had been neatly tucked under it. She looked like Medusa as the dim light from the flashlight highlighted the snakes of hair surrounding her face.

The rustling increased. I heard what sounded like a thousand little clicking noises growing in volume as a cloud of pulsating blackness came out of the pitch dark.

"This is dangerous, Aunt Maggie!" I shouted. "I'm not standing here, and neither are you!" I grabbed Maggie by the shoulders, preparing to pick her up and carry her out if necessary.

"It might be a spirit of the dead!" she warbled, above the din.

"Or it might be the spirit of something alive," I countered.

I turned her around, and we ran as the flashlight beam bobbed against the walls. I could feel something pulling at my hair and reached up to grab it. When I did, a Mexican bat flapped out of my grasp. We careened out the door and slammed it behind us. We could hear the thud of a few bats hitting the door and then what sounded like the wings of hundreds of bats flapping as they turned back down the tunnel.

I turned around to see Maggie, leaning against the wall, trying to push the hair out of her face and catch her breath. "Are you all right?" I asked, as we both panted at each other.

"Yes, a little jittery, but I'll be fine."

"Maggie? Betsy?" A voice came toward us from the other end of the hallway. It was Howard. He was in his late fifties with straight silver hair that was a little too long. When the wind caught it, the thin strands would blow in wisps, reminding me of puppets on children's television. He was wearing a flowered Hawaiian shirt, brown corduroy shorts and hiking boots.

"I thought I heard a scream. Isn't that exciting? Quite possibly we are in an area of high paranormal activity."

"Before you get too high on anything there, Howard, the scream you heard was of this world, not the next," I said.

"You had a sighting then?"

"Not exactly," I continued, as my breathing steadied. "We were down the dead tunnel and got rushed by probably a hundred or so bats."

Howard walked over to the door we had just so ceremoniously slammed shut. He nodded his head in the affirmative. "Good to know. I'll need to make sure the film crew knows about the bats when we start filming down the dead tunnel. We'll be filming at night, and as you know, bats are nocturnal and will probably be out on their evening hunt."

I reflected again on the name of the passageway from which I had just escaped. Funny how nobody seems to mention a name like that until you get near the tunnel. After my recent experience with it, I wasn't so sure ghost hunting was for me. This was the paranormal experience more suited for seasoned investigators who wanted the bejeezus scared out of them. It was not for someone like me, who now totally owned up to the whole chicken thing.

"Aunt Maggie, I don't think I can go back down that tunnel again. Is there somewhere we can check out that's not quite so creepy?"

Howard glared. "Being a paranormal investigator is not for the faint of heart. I thought Maggie explained to you that we could be crossing into worlds unknown."

Great. First I get rushed by bats, and now a lecture from "Dr. Who Took My Brain."

"You got me, Howard. When it comes to ghost hunting, I'm just an amateur."

"Come on, Howard," Maggie said. "Give the kid a break. It is creepy down that dead tunnel. I think we need a bigger team than just the two of us. How's about we go to a nice, open place like the solarium upstairs? Not so claustrophobic, and there might be some lingering spirits up there. That was probably one of the places people were happiest here."

Yay for my Aunt Maggie for coming up with that one.

"You have a point," Howard conceded. "It might have been an uplifting experience for the patients, producing a positive energy dynamic for the spirits."

With Howard's blessing, we headed up the creaking stairs to the second level of the hospital. As we ascended, a smothering heat came upon us. I sure hoped some of these lingering spirits had brought a fan with them.

"Hot enough for ya?" Maggie said. In Pecan Bayou, this phrase was Texan for "Hello" and could easily be exchanged at any time for "How do you do?" or "Have a nice day."

We came to a long open room, one side banked in windows. A few rusty bed frames still stood against the opposite wall. Thinking about the stifling heat, I wondered how anyone would want to be in this room in the days before air conditioning. There were plenty of windows to allow for a cross breeze, but on a day like today, any breeze was rare. We shuffled along as my aunt looked up and around. I think she was expecting a full-fledged apparition to pop up in front of her.

"This was the sun porch," Howard said. "They believed lots of sunshine could cure TB. Crazy today. Many people passed on in these rooms. We are thick with paranormal activity here." He waved around a little metal device that looked like a phaser from Star Trek.

"What are you doing?" I asked.

"I'm measuring the EMF readings. Paranormal beings emit electrical signals that can be picked up."

"Not good if you're ghost huntin' at the power company though," Aunt Maggie said.

Even though there was plenty of light up here, I couldn't shake the dead tunnel out of my mind. I felt like backing up, not crunching forward following Maggie and Howard through the scattered papers, broken plaster and shredded wallpaper.

Howard continued with what was turning into a walking tour of the old place. "The town built this hospital back in 1911 when tuberculosis was called 'consumption.' The building could house one hundred patients."

"Did many people die?" I asked.

"If someone was diagnosed with tuberculosis, they were required to stay at a hospital for three to five years. During that period, maybe ten out of a hundred people might die, so it wasn't necessarily a death sentence," Howard said.

I reached out and touched a rusty sign. "Hmm, no smoking. It's a wonder they even had to put that up in a tuberculosis hospital," I said.

"In the beginning they didn't even know smokin' was bad for you. They probably put it up because the smoke made the sheets stink," Aunt Maggie said.

We looked down the hall at the doors lined up like old soldiers waiting for their assignments. It was like some kind of macabre bedroom farce movie. In my mind, I could see spirits running in and out of the barely hinged doors hanging from the doorways. Aunt Maggie fingered the tiny cross at her neck.

"When I looked at the old blueprints," Maggie said, "I saw a room up here that would be perfect for the angle of the cameras and what light we can produce. We can run an electric cord right out the window to the van below."

We walked down the hallway, which was spray-painted with more graffiti and littered with torn-off strips of wallpaper.

"What would it have been like to have to stay in this place for five years? No family, no home. It must have been very lonely," I said.

We walked to Room 227 at the end of the hall. There was an overwhelming stench that seemed to permeate the air both inside the room and out in the hallway. Upon entering 227, I saw it was a corner room with windows on two sides. I stuck my head out of one window and saw dried-out vines, all brown and crunchy, climbing up the side of the building. The windows had long since broken, and nature was taking over this little corner. I pulled my head back in to feel the odor creeping into my nostrils again.

"What stinks?" I said.

"I don't know. Seems like something died," Maggie answered.

"Lots of things died here, but this seems a little fresher." The rotting smell mixed with heat was becoming overpowering.

There was one piece of furniture in the room, an old dresser, that didn't look like the fiberboard wonders available down at SuperWally. Always wanting to be on the Antiques Roadshow, I held my nose and went over and gave it my best unofficial expert look-over.

"Howard, help me turn this dresser around so I can see if there is a name anywhere on it. It looks like it's from the '20s. I think it used to be white. Look at the little legs and the woodwork on the bottom. Too bad a drawer is missing at the top."

Howard walked over and tried to wiggle one side of the dresser to pull it away from the wall. He couldn't get it to budge.

"Hmm." My eyes scanned up and down the front for a manufacturer's name or the date when it was made. "Doesn't have any markings."

Just as Howard and I were about to free the dresser from the spot where it had probably sat for decades, we heard a noise outside which sounded like someone was walking across the gravel in front of the hospital.

Maggie looked out the window, carefully dodging the broken panes of glass. "That's funny," she said. "Howard, do we have a new member of the paranormal society? A woman? She's nosin' around out there looking through the windows."

"I wasn't aware of another member. Perhaps the word of mouth got around about our trip into the unknown. You never know who will get the call to the world of spirits."

A woman was pacing around in the weeds below, dressed in a dark blue gabardine suit and flat heels. All she needed was a string of pearls to complete her look. She looked as if she had lost someone.

"Excuse me," Aunt Maggie yelled out. "Are you looking for someone?"

The woman, who had been unaware of our presence upstairs, jumped back.

"Um ... no," she answered. She must have thought we were the lingering spirits. She patted her head to straighten the perma-tight hairdo that lay perfectly in set curls on the back of her head. "May I ask who you are?"

"We are members of the Pecan Bayou Paranormal Society," Maggie yelled out. "We are doing extensive ghost huntin' investigations throughout the entire hospital, and it will be televised on NUTV."

"Paranormal? And you are walking through the entire hospital? The hospital will be the subject of a television program?"

"Pretty near."

Howard popped his head out of the window next to Maggie. "Do you wish to join our group in a search for the paranormal?"

The woman looked up, shading the sun from her eyes, not seeming to register Howard's kind invitation to join us loonies. Not getting an immediate response from her, Howard continued. "Or were you here for some other reason?"

"I'm ... I'm ..." She rubbed her brow and straightened the oversized glasses resting on her jutting cheekbones. She reminded me of a schoolmarm shutting the door of the classroom as she reined in her students after a long, carefree summer. She continued, now finding a firmer voice. "I find the presence of a group who chooses to dabble in the occult, right here in our town, outrageous!"

The woman seemed to be composing herself as she began shaking a long, thin finger upwards at us. "You are inciting the evil of this place. Come out now."

"Oh dear," said Maggie as she looked over the windowsill. "This can't be good for our investigation."

"I don't see how it could help," I added. The woman standing below us started backing up a little, still shading her eyes as she tried to focus on us. I now noticed a neat, green Ford parked in the gravel lot in front of the hospital. I was surprised we hadn't heard her pull up, but then we were busy being swarmed by bats.

"You people are trespassing on this property." She pulled a cell phone out of the front seat of her car. "I am calling the police."

"Whoa, ma'am. That's a little extreme isn't it?" Howard said.

I watched her punch in the number as I wondered if she had the police on speed dial for incidents such as this one.

"Good luck with gettin' us arrested, my dear. The officer who will probably respond to your call is related to two of us," Maggie said.

We were all leaned out the windows as we watched her report our trespass to the Pecan Bayou Police Department. I guess when the paranormal is involved, the zealots come out of the woodwork. I just wouldn't have expected anyone out here so quickly. If I remembered right, my dad had said he would be over at the new hospital this afternoon going through hurricane procedures with the chief of staff. He would be tickled pink to hear about this.

I turned back to see Howard pushing buttons on his own cell phone.

"If we're going to get into trouble, I better let Stan Gibson at NUTV know about it before he cancels the filming." Howard stepped out into the hallway, narrowly missing the door hanging from one hinge.

In a few short minutes, my father rolled up through the gravel in his squad car. Homeland Security might have given up on the color-coded alert system, but the many shades of red my father's face could take on were a true barometer of any impending crisis. As he looked up and determined we were the cause of his disturbance, his skin tone was somewhere between watermelon pink and fire engine red. That would mean his reaction would be somewhere between "Can I help you?" and "What the hell is going on here?" Why were people so concerned about an old, dilapidated building? Maggie couldn't wait to get in here and find ghosts, and other people, like this woman, seemed to be terrified of it. The woman below stamped over to my father's police car.

"Officer, you have to get these people out of this building immediately. The citizens of this town do not want them meddling with witchcraft and broadcasting it on television. Who would want to invest in this property or even move to this town once they knew that it is full of people who worship the occult? Tell me that! It's just disgusting what little minds resort to."

Maggie bristled at the little part, pulling herself up to her full four-foot-eight.

"Excuse me ma'am," my father said, pulling a small notebook from the pocket of his shirt. "I didn't catch your name."

"My name," she stood up straight as if to announce it to a large crowd, "is Maureen Boyle, and I didn't tell you my name."

"Yes, Mrs. Boyle."

"Miss Boyle!" She peered at the badge pinned to his shirt. "I will be recording your badge number. What is your name, sir?"

"My name is Lieutenant Juddson Kelsey, ma'am," he said in his most placating voice. Funny how I never heard much of that voice at home growing up, but he did seem to use it well on crazy ladies.

"Miss Boyle," he drawled — pure Texas — with a deliberate slowness over her last name. "Miss Boyle, what these people are doing here is with the permission of the town."

"Just who in the town granted this permission?"

"Well ... my boss, the chief of police. And I'm sure it's fine with just about anyone on the town council."

"So, Lieutenant Kelsey, there was a meeting of the town council granting this film crew permission to create a ghost-hunting program in this building?"

"Not in so many words, but they pretty well all know about it."

Miss Boyle put her hand up to her throat, reminding me of a turkey neck at Thanksgiving. "Pretty well? Was there or was there not a meeting and a vote to allow this investigation to take place?"

My father sighed. "There wasn't one I was aware of."

"Ah ha!" snapped Miss Boyle. "I thought not."

"But I think they all know about the program, and a couple of them are even excited about seeing it."

"Sir, this is a clear case of town officials acting in their own interest and not the interest of the people they are supposed to be representing," Miss Boyle said.

"Miss Boyle, most people in this town are too busy trying to figure out how to put food on the table, and they really don't care all that much about anything going on in this old place."

Miss Boyle raised her head and gazed into the broken windows of the hospital, and then she looked down her nose at my father. "You speak for the town now, do you? Well, I can assure you, you don't speak for me, sir." Miss Boyle looked up at Maggie, who was leaning against the peeling paint of the second-floor window. "The good people of this town might be a little concerned knowing about this pack of charlatans out here."

"That's enough," my father said, losing his gentle tone. "Miss Boyle, perhaps you can tell me just what *you* are doing out here."

"That, sir, is none of your business."

"Well, from where I stand, your presence out here is not all that different from our friends upstairs, so I think it is my business."

Miss Boyle straightened her shoulders and tossed her cell phone back into her car. She jutted her chin out. "I am leaving, officer, as I can clearly see I am outnumbered here, and you are siding with them."

"I am not siding with them, ma'am. It is just that the paranormal group isn't hurting anyone, and you are disturbing their peace."

"Disturbing their peace?" Her face went the color of a deep red communion wine. "Disturbing their peace? Well, I never! You will be hearing from me sir." She scooted behind the wheel of her car. "This is far from over, Lieutenant." She slammed the door shut. My dad watched her drive off, putting his notepad back into the front pocket of his navy blue cotton police uniform.

"Thank you, Judd," my aunt said.

"Hey Dad," I said as Ms. Boyle's car skittered gravel behind her. "Dad, maybe you ought to come up here. There is a pretty bad smell coming from somewhere."

"Like what?" he shouted back.

"Like dead things," Maggie answered.

"This old building is probably crawling with rats. I expect there's a dead one in the wall, that's all. On my way." I turned back and remembered the dresser we had been about to move. Howard was back in from his phone call.

"Let's look at the back of this dresser, Howard."

"So we can find a dead rat for your father to arrest?"

"Hopefully not. I just wanted to see if there was a date or a name on the back of this thing. It might be worth a lot of money," I answered.

Howard stuck his phone in his pocket and walked over. Putting our hands on the sides of the dresser, we both pushed. As the ancient legs screeched across the floor, the smell increased tenfold. Once the dresser was moved, I could see a large hole punched out of the drywall, obscured by the dresser. Ragged edges of plaster and lumber stuck out of the hole.

"Good God," said Maggie, "that's awful." The odor came at us full force. I expected Howard to be all over this, but the paranormal aficionado seemed to be backing away from it.

I held my nose again and leaned over to put my head into to the hole. It was dark, but from the sparse light that filtered in from the outer room, I could see a large closet-type space. "Aunt Maggie, hand me your flashlight."

"Here ya go." She stuck her arm out and extended it as far as it would go, giving me the red plastic utility flashlight. I was sure my father was wandering around downstairs. He was probably trying to remember where the stairway was from his last disturbance call to this hospital.

I clicked the flashlight on and focused the beam around the dusty inner room.

"What do you see?" asked Maggie.

"A bunch of old whiskey bottles. Happy hour for the ghosts, I guess."

"More like happy hour for the workers here. Some of those bottles may be worth more than this tacky dresser. It was a marvelous hideaway. An orderly could climb in, take a nip, climb out, return the dresser to its place and no one would know the better."

There was dust dancing through the beam of my flashlight. This was probably a ventilation shaft in the building. I could see on one end of the room what looked like another tunnel leading somewhere else. There were exposed pipes and cobwebs throughout the dusty space. This was the inner structure of the building. I held my breath and stepped through the hole until I stood completely in the makeshift hideaway. The stench was even more powerful, and I felt my stomach lurch. Quite possibly a rat and his entire family had come in here to die. As long as I didn't breathe through my nose, I could stop the contents of my stomach from rising up. I explored with the light to the farthest point in the room. I saw what looked like an old suit balled up in the corner. As I bounced the light beam across it, I could see the pile was much more than a suit. I stepped closer and felt something sticky under my feet. It was hard to believe that whiskey spilled in here decades ago would still be sticky. I edged closer to the pile of clothes as the odor seemed to be hitting me in waves. Covering my nose and mouth with my hand and stood in front of the discarded suit. As I looked at a tilted shoe, I saw a leg sticking in it. It was then I realized there was a man in the crumpled suit, and he was dead.

CHAPTER FIVE

AN HOUR LATER, THE quiet – if not slightly haunted – tuberculosis hospital was abuzz with activity. Aunt Maggie and I watched Art Rivera, the county coroner and my dad's poker buddy, load the body in the suit onto a gurney.

"Thanks, Art, we have all we need here. I'll be down your way when you get the autopsy complete," my dad said, as he looked through the dead man's trifold brown leather wallet.

"Sure enough," the coroner answered. Art had moved up from Harris County in Houston, looking forward to a lighter workload. He told my father he had seen way too many murders down in the Bayou City that he would rather forget. Now, having time to bait some hooks was a pretty decent remedy for all he had seen. Art's wife had not been too crazy about moving, but when their grown children had spread out from Corpus Christi to San Antonio, Pecan Bayou seemed like a great place to bring the grandkids. The police department was happy to have an experienced coroner at the county level.

"We ought to have this one finished right before Halloween. That'll put you in the haunting mood."

"Always does," said my dad with a twinkle in his eye. He turned to Maggie and me, now sitting on the recently dusted windowsills. "So, ladies, it seems our dead man was Oliver Canfield."

"Oliver Canfield?" I stood up from the windowsill and took the wallet from my father. There, smiling up at me from the driver's license, was the one and only partner of my missing husband.

"I thought he closed up the office and left town after Barry disappeared," I said.

"I'll have to check it out. I didn't know he was back in Pecan Bayou either."

"Oh my." Maggie clucked her tongue. She glanced at the driver's license I was holding up and bit her bottom lip.

"Well, what would he be doing out here?" I asked.

"Maybe he was going to try to sell the place," said Maggie. "Somebody with a lot of elbow grease could fix this place up and make it into a spa or something."

I shook my head. "A lot of elbow grease and a lot of money. This place is falling apart, Maggie. It would be cheaper just to pull the whole building down and start again." One thing I was proficient at was money – spending it, making it and saving it.

"I suppose you're right. I can always count on you to find out how much a thing would cost, Betsy," she said.

"I would love it if someone would do something with this place," said my dad. "Seems like we get a call to come out here about once a month because some group of juvenile delinquents is out here havin' a party or smokin' something funny. Just look at all the graffiti on these walls. This is years and years of nuisance calls. Last year I was called out on Halloween because someone was holding some sort of seance just down the hall. The year before that, kids were drinkin' and jumpin' out of the second-story window. Don't know what it is, but people get into this ol' place and just forget how to think straight."

"You can't deny the paranormal element surrounding us, Lieutenant Kelsey." Howard spoke up from where he had been quietly standing against the back wall, holding a white handkerchief up to his mouth. He was starting to look a little green. "There are malevolent spirits here."

"The malevolence here is purely human. A bad act by a bad person."

"Maybe Canfield was looking at the property and met up with a crazy person or something," I said, now looking again at Canfield's ID. The face was familiar, but I remembered him with thinner jowls. Seven years ago I had listened daily to Barry's plans, always centered around his business with Canfield Investments. To me, Oliver Canfield was the guy who had led Barry into all the crummy deals he made and instilled in him the belief that living above your means was perfectly natural. He advocated the style of living that I had to pay off after Barry skipped town. What a despicable man he was. I didn't even know this guy anymore, and even I had a motive for killing him. I could remember sitting at the dinner table with him and Barry, listening to all of their dreams and schemes for hitting it big. They were going to be rich. Rich, as long as it involved other people's money.

Aunt Maggie gently touched my arm. She could pretty well feel where my mind was going. "He must have met up with someone out here. Still pushin' those great investment deals."

George Beckman, another officer on the Pecan Bayou police force, had been working behind us and now handed my father a folded piece of paper with a spot of blood on the bottom of it. George was a burly man who scared most of the Texas country boys in town right up until he opened his mouth. For a burly man, he had an uncharacteristically high voice. "Take a look at this," he squeaked.

Dad carefully unfolded the paper and adjusted the glasses on the end of his nose as he read. "It seems Mr. Canfield here had an agreement with Benny Mason, the owner of Benny's Barbecue. Canfield was about to take fifty percent of the profit startin' the first of November." I remembered the photograph I saw in Benny's restaurant. Now I recognized who was helping him cut the ribbon – Oliver Canfield.

"Why would he do that?" I asked.

"According to the contract, it's to pay back a loan made between the two parties."

"Benny?" I said. "You're kidding me. That can't be right. I don't know what kind of trouble he's gotten himself into, but he surely wouldn't go murdering anyone."

"You never know, darlin'. I've seen all kinds of people end up doing crimes you'd never expect. Benny certainly had a motive, but I'll also check around to see if anyone reported seeing any vagrants out here. You know the new hospital is right down the road. Maybe someone saw something or someone who didn't belong over here," my father added.

"He riled somebody up, that's for sure," Maggie said.

"Well, until I get this all figured out, I think this room and possibly the entire hospital needs to be shut down to outsiders," my father announced.

Howard's bushy silver eyebrows lifted. "Outsiders not meaning us, correct, Sheriff?"

"Outsiders meaning everyone but the police."

"Judd," Maggie pleaded. She put her hands on her hips and faced him. I knew being denied access to the hospital by her little brother wasn't flying with her. "This is the biggest event the paranormal society has ever done. We have planned it for over a year. You just can't stop it now."

"Maggie." My father's voice edged with aggravation. "I can, and I will. This place could be dangerous, and if there is a killer walking around, I certainly am not going to have my family out here."

Maggie's face clouded. I knew, even more than my father, how important this investigation was to her. I had been over to her house and seen the television tuned endlessly to ghost-hunting programs. She had become interested in the paranormal after my Uncle Jeeter died and would be utterly crushed if she couldn't do this thing. Maggie didn't ask much out of us. She had always been there for me and Zach. I knew if I could figure out what was going on out here myself, I might be able to give back a little.

I walked back to the hole in the wall as my father, my aunt and Howard continued arguing over the use of the hospital. George Beckman left the room, probably to get more evidence bags. My father could be pigheaded sometimes, and I knew he would get a strange little joy out of keeping his older sister out of his business.

"Betsy, stay away from that area. It's a crime scene." I jumped at his command, amazed he knew I had decided to play Nancy Drew.

"I didn't touch anything, Dad," I answered. Lying here on the floor had been the one man who could have solved my own mystery. What did he know about Barry? Did he know where he went? Did he have something to do with his disappearance? Had he killed him and left his body somewhere? It seemed so unfair that I finally had a lead on my own husband's disappearance and it seemed to be slipping out of my grasp.

He shook his head. "Thank you for not touching anything, and that is all the more reason I'm clearing you people out of here."

"Judd!" Maggie was getting mad. "We will do our investigation with or without your blessing. This is a big building, and there are other areas we could use without tromping across your crime scene."

"That is correct, sir," Howard said. "When there is a crime in an apartment building, you don't force all of the other tenants to move."

He had my dad on that one.

"Well, for right now, I'm telling you all to move."

"Judd!" My aunt was not letting go of this one.

"Okay, Maggie. We'll compromise. I'll post George here at the crime scene until after Halloween, and you can have the run of the hospital. That suit ya?"

"Suits me fine." Maggie smiled and crossed her arms.

CHAPTER SIX

THAT EVENING, AS I sat in Zach's Texas Scout meeting, I was surprised to see Benny, ever faithful, leading his Scout troop. I knew he had spent a couple of hours in my father's office that afternoon, a fate I wouldn't wish on anybody. Other than a slightly worried look and his request I not tell the Scouts about the interview, he seemed normal. Hearing that it might be Benny Mason who killed Oliver Canfield just wasn't ringing true with me. If I had to pick the town murderer, it never would have been him. Every time I was in the barbecue place there were other customers coming and going. It seemed to be a profitable business. I was thankful for Benny's male influence in Zach's life and the fact that he would let Zach be a part of his crew when the Scouts scheduled the many father/son campouts. Was this another lesson life had for me in trusting the wrong person?

I was sitting in a folding chair, crowded in with the rest of the parents as I watched my son playing a relay game with the other Scouts. Zach, who was smaller than many of the boys, was running as fast as his little legs would take him. He was laughing as he and his friends attempted to beat the other team. I worried about his broken arm, but he had adapted to the cast quickly and now didn't even seem to notice it. The din of the boyhood yells was deafening.

Zach was now second in line to run the relay. In front of him stood a stocky kid that I hadn't seen before, wearing a crisp new Scout uniform. He ran his hand through his dark brown hair to push it out of his eyes. Was he from the older group of boys? Why was he competing with Zach's group of skinnier, less coordinated boys? It's like when Zach would get in one of those inflatable bounce houses and a whopping big kid would get in and jump all over him. The boy in front of Zach burst out from the line and ran across the open area. On his way back, he began to wobble and couldn't stop. He plowed into Zach, who was at the front of the line, flattening him onto the tile floor. I cringed when I saw the cast hit the floor, hoping we wouldn't be running to the emergency room tonight.

I raced toward them, seeing Benny hurrying over from the other side. Zach scrambled up, stood on his tiptoes and pushed the boy on the shoulder. The big kid pushed him right back, causing Zach to lose his footing. He pulled himself back up and began exchanging words, although I couldn't make out what was said. Benny and I made it over just in time to hear the other boy yell, "Oh, right. So where is your dad? Huh? Huh?"

Benny grabbed both boys by the scruff of the neck. Zach was hanging from his Scoutmaster's hold, his little fist swinging at the larger boy. The other boy was probably fifty pounds heavier than Zach, and no doubt he could pound my little guy to the ground in nothing flat. Unfortunately, that didn't seem to matter to Zach. He was really, really mad at the kid. He reminded me of Aunt Maggie fighting my dad.

"I said that's enough!" commanded Benny.

"Zach!" I said. "Settle down!"

"Mom, this boy knocked me down and said bad stuff about Dad." I had never seen this kid before until tonight. How could he know about our history with my absent husband? It was unreal how fast gossip traveled in this town and just who heard it. I looked over at the boy, who now shifted his eyes down but still held onto a chuckle and a smirk.

"Tyler!"

I jumped as another man seemed to have appeared out of nowhere. He was tall, about six feet, and lanky. "What is going on here, son?"

The boy glanced at Zach and then quietly yet defiantly said, "Nothing."

"You were about to hit this boy, Tyler. It can't be nothing."

Zach piped up to the stranger, ready to defend his case. "He was saying bad stuff about my dad."

"Is that true, Tyler?"

"No sir," Tyler answered, like a marine recruit.

"That's not true!" Zach screamed out.

"Tyler, did you say something about this boy's father?"

"His dad took a powder years ago, and everyone knows it. What's the matter – need your daddy?" Tyler mocked.

"Excuse me," I couldn't take this anymore. This kid was outrageous. The tall man's glance shifted towards me.

"Ma'am." He nodded.

"I am Zachary's mother. Is this your son?"

"Uh, yes it is. Tyler here was just about to apologize for insulting your husband."

"Zachary's father is ... not in the picture ... but I will listen to the apology." I struggled to get the words out. It's one thing for the town to talk about me and my absent husband, but to go after a little kid was unthinkable.

Benny helped out. "Mrs. Livingston is one of our single parents in the Scout troop."

The tall man then took his burly son and held him in front of him, in a gentle, yet sturdy restraint. "I'm so sorry, Mrs. Livingston." Tyler muttered an apology after his dad.

I looked at him in amazement. Was he sorry I was a single parent and that my husband took a powder, or was he sorry that his meathead of a son had just bashed mine both physically and emotionally?

He realized how that had sounded. "I mean ... well ... I'm sorry for Tyler's behavior towards your son. My name is Leo Fitzpatrick, and we are new in town. Actually, we're new at everything. Tyler has just come to live with me. His mother was raising him, but ..."

He seemed uncomfortable all of a sudden and paused as if in thought but then continued. "She has remarried and asked me to take Tyler for a while. That being said, discipline is an issue we are presently working on."

"Da-ad," Tyler looked up and whined a bit. "What I said was just what the guys were saying. They said this kid's dad was missing and that his mom found him at the old hospital today."

Zach gasped and looked at me his eyes now wide. "You found Dad today?"

"Zach ..." I stuttered. I hadn't intended on telling him anything about what happened out at the old hospital.

"You found Dad? Was he ... Did he have ... cough drops with him?" Tyler exploded into giggles and met the eyes of several of the other boys, who also started laughing.

"Zach." I knelt down to his level. "Zach, I did find a man today who ... had passed on. The man I found was not your dad. It was a man named Oliver Canfield."

Zach's eyes searched me for reassurance. "You promise? It wasn't Dad? You wouldn't just say that?"

"No, if it had been Dad, I would have told you right away." I put my arm around him and sat him in a folding chair. His bottom lip puckered out, and he put his elbows on his knees.

"I really wish you'd found my dad today ... alive."

"I know you did, but I promise, it wasn't him."

Zach's shoulders slumped. I could see tears attempting to escape from his eyes. Tyler, whose father had his hand on his shoulder started to pull away from him. Mr. Fitzpatrick pulled him back.

"No more fighting, do you hear me?"

Tyler's reply was soft but laced with underlying rage. "I hear you."

This kid was even a bully to his own father. I would not want to see him in a few years when the hormones hit and teenage rebellion set in full force. He snapped away from his father and became aware of my watchful presence. Tyler looked over at Zach in tears and then smiled, still enjoying his pain. He ran off to the other Scouts who had now restarted the relay. His father, Fitzpatrick, put his hands in his pockets and ambled over to Zach and me sitting in the chairs.

"Sorry about that," he said. "Did you say Oliver Canfield?"

"Yes, I didn't know it was him at first, but then my dad, who is on the police force, let me have a look at his ID."

"Oliver Canfield, the investment guy?"

"That's the one. Why, do you know him?"

"I met him briefly out on the grounds of that old hospital. I was out there doing some scouting for an investor I represent from Dallas. We were thinking of doing something with the property. What a wreck that old place is. Anyway, I was out there walking around, and I heard someone clear their throat. It nearly scared me to death. I turned around, and there was Mr. Canfield." He paused, debating whether or not to say his next comment. He leaned in closer to me. "I think that guy was just a little bit ... shady, if you know what I mean."

"Yes, I'd have to agree with you on that. When did you run into him?"

He sighed and lightly tugged at the collar of his steam-pressed shirt. He looked like the kind of guy who drops his shirts off at the laundry rather than ironing them at home. "I don't know, maybe Tuesday, maybe Wednesday. That place is really creepy. To be honest, when I first saw him, I thought I was seeing a ghost or something. We, uh, laughed about it," Mr. Fitzpatrick said.

"Was there anyone else there with him?"

"No, I didn't see anybody. He did seem a little nervous about being there. I guess that old place had him jumpy. There are so many rooms; a person could get lost without a map. How long has it been vacant?"

"Um ... I guess it's been about thirty or forty years."

"I can't believe someone hasn't tried to develop the site before this."

"This is a small town, Mr. Fitzpatrick. Not like Dallas. A commercial investment like a mall or a sports complex would require lots of customers to keep going."

He looked around the room at the scattering of Scouts and parents. "Yes, I see what you mean."

"Well, welcome to Pecan Bayou."

"Thank you, but now that I know there's been a murder out at the hospital, I don't think your chamber of commerce wants to advertise there are some real nuts along with the pecans residing here."

CHAPTER SEVEN

THE NEXT DAY, AFTER practically bribing Zach to go to school after the Scout incident, I drove around trying to find a parking spot in front of the Birdies Diner. I was here to do a book talk today for the ladies' book club from the Baptist church. I had a packed suitcase full of paperback copies of my helpful hints book and was ready to educate them with "Hints to Help Them in Their Daily Lives." I just hoped I could live up to their expectations.

Pecan Bayou was starting to resemble a cheesy horror movie with all of its Halloween finery stapled and taped on every doorway, lamppost and window. There was a ghoul with crazy hair hanging in the window of The Best Little Hair House (probably not the best marketing gimmick) and construction paper pumpkins taped up in the windows of Buzz Aldrin Elementary School. One of those pumpkins was most probably made by my own son, who was also probably sitting sullenly in his desk right now, wishing the day would end.

Some of the store owners had nailed up purple and green blinking lights, and a few were channeling ghostly sounds out of their front speakers. People in this town loved Halloween. I always wondered whether the appeal was the opportunity to dress up and be somebody different or the consumption of mass amounts of sugar.

Our town had its own distinct personality. Pecan Bayou was just north and west of Houston. Compared to the big city, it could feel like an island of peace. Snow was a once-a-year thing, and you haven't lived until you've tasted German potato salad with a little hot sauce added.

The population represented a strange mix of cultures. German and Czechoslovakian immigrants settled this area, and we were a part of Texas' fight for independence. Sam Houston slept here, and Santa Anna's troops killed here. Pecan Bayou was famous for its wildflowers in the spring. Tourists would drive along the highways and country roads to enjoy the bursts of purple petals, the oranges of Indian paintbrushes and the ever-true Texas bluebonnets. All of this was thanks to Lady Bird Johnson, who beautified highways all over the state by planting wildflowers. Every spring the medians on the interstates and in the towns were left uncut to produce a beautiful array of floral wonders.

As I parked my station wagon in front of the Birdies Diner, I heard a distinct clunking sound in the motor. Maybe I pumped some bad gas the last time I filled up the tank. I had driven this station wagon for eight years now and intended to drive it until the wheels fell off. I hoped today wasn't the day. I heard "The Eyes of Texas Are Upon You" playing from my purse — my cell phone. I had assigned that ringtone to my father, whose eyes were always on this town. I pulled the phone out of my bulging black bag as the familiar "Dad" flashed on the illuminated panel.

"Betsy, I thought you'd like to know we have a preliminary report from the coroner's office." I shut off the air conditioning and immediately felt the car starting to heat up like a sauna. The weather today was stuffy, and even though we were close to the end of hurricane season, it sure felt like the unease that precedes a whopper of a storm. I opened the door to try to catch a cool draft and circulate some air. The heat rushed in instead, disguised as my sought-after breeze.

"Oh good. Tell me that you have nothing that connects Benny."

"Darlin', I'm still checking his alibi out. He says he was out in the woods next to the hospital finding the best site to set up the Scout tents."

"Was anybody with him?"

"Now that would be too easy." My dad's voice crackled on the other end. "No, he was alone, and that puts our favorite barbecue king next to a murder scene."

Having your dad working for the police department could be a blessing and curse all at the same time. He could be disagreeable and stubborn, which made him an outstanding police officer, but every once in a while his soft side would show, much to his dismay. He wouldn't let me date until I was sixteen, and even then he followed along behind us in his squad car. It was a little intimidating for any young man. When he found out my husband had skipped town, he put a dragnet out on the guy. It was one of the few cases he hadn't solved. He had worked as a lieutenant to our police chief, Arvin Wilson, for the last decade. Time spent on a small-town police force could make a man cynical and not as trusting as the rest of us. I loved my dad and all the things he was for me and Zach, but still I wouldn't want to be on the wrong side of the law from him. He had worked a few murder cases in the past that were mostly the result of domestic disturbances and some "good ol' boys gone bad." An all-out whodunit was probably a welcome challenge for him. His voice on the other end interrupted my thoughts.

"Mr. Canfield was shot."

"Shot?"

"Yes. Three times, to be exact. He was shot twice in the chest and once in the head. I'm figuring our killer shot him at point-blank range, and then when Canfield fell face down, he finished him off with a shot to the back of the head."

"It's hard to believe somebody around here did that."

"I agree. We probably need to look at strangers in town, that sort of thing, first."

"Speaking of strangers, I met one at Zach's scout meeting." I explained to my father about the fight over my missing husband.

"That's my boy," he chuckled. "Don't take guff off of anybody."

"That's *our* boy," I echoed. "The bully kid had a new dad who was a little out of his league in the parenting department. That kid didn't seem to care much about anything. Anyway, this boy's father told me that he actually ran into Canfield out at the hospital on the day he was murdered."

"Is that right?"

"Yes. He said he was scouting the property for an investment company, and it seems Canfield was doing the same kind of thing. He talked like Canfield might have creeped him out a bit."

"Why is that?"

"I don't know. He just sort of caught a vibe." I knew my dad loved the "vibe" school of investigation.

"Uh huh." He paused but then let himself agree with my theory. "Maybe Canfield had something sneaky going on."

"Or maybe the boy's father did," I answered, now thinking that sitting in a hot car even with the door open was not a good idea.

"Well, it could be like father, like son. Any kid who goes after Zach starts out in the hole with me. Thanks for letting me know, Betsy. You think you can get a phone number for this guy? I'd like to talk with him. Oh, and one more thing, Canfield had oil lubricant on his hands. Did the boy's father mention anything about him holding an oil can, or maybe oiling some hinges or something?"

"No, but we didn't go into that much detail. He just said he had been looking around the hospital and ran into him."

"Well, he didn't have a lot on his hands. Curiously it was just on his little finger."

I thought about that. "His little finger, like on the fingertip where he might be applying oil onto something?"

"No, up near where the finger connects to the hand. Like maybe it splashed on his hand. It was found on the palm and the back side of the finger."

I didn't think Canfield moonlighted as a mechanic, although from what I knew of him, a few shady repair jobs wouldn't be below him. I remembered Celia's ring not fitting on her finger anymore.

"Dad, could it be the murderer pulled a ring off his finger?"

"Maybe, although I'm not thinking robbery was the motive, because there was money in his wallet." He paused for a moment as I could tell he was reading through the report. "One other thing, there was some sort of concrete mixture on his clothes."

"Like someone broke a concrete block on him?"

"Like he had just mixed up some concrete."

"In a suit?" What had this guy been doing? First the oil, and then the concrete.

"We found his address. He had a place over in Andersonville. We couldn't find any new patches of concrete. We found evidence of it on his palm and jacket sleeve."

I looked up into the window of Birdies Diner, and some of the members of my ladies group inside the diner were now waving at me through the glass. I opened the back seat door and pulled out my rolling bag of extra book copies.

"Dad, I have to go."

"OK, think about the concrete. What would he have been doing?"

"I have no idea, but it seems like a strange thing to do dressed in a suit at an abandoned hospital."

I put my cell phone back in my purse, closed the car door and waved at the smiling ladies. There were purple lights blinking on the door around a laughing jack-o-lantern that also seemed to be smiling at me.

Feeling the heat press in, I took off the brown denim jacket that I had intended to wear for my presentation. I had tried to look businesslike but already felt as if I were wilting from the morning heat. Everywhere else in the country, people were getting out their sweaters and coats. South Texans were wondering if our flip-flops could last just a few more weeks.

I carried along my laptop with my database of hints in it for the unusual "hint" questions I would get. After visiting the tuberculosis hospital and stepping in the blood, maybe I should look up how to get bloodstains out of clothing.

Jackie Bryant greeted me as I came through the door. She was running the diner for her mom, Birdie, who was out of state for a few weeks. Jackie had been a high school classmate of mine. We had never been close friends, but after Barry left, she was the first person to tell me, as she put it, "Marriage is like a phone call at night – first the ring, and then you wake up." She had "woken up" already with a divorce in her early twenties after learning her husband was cheating on her with an old girlfriend from Longview. She knew what I was going through, and I was lucky to have her to talk to.

In the next half hour, I talked a little bit about the book and was just answering a question on washing tennis shoes when Leo Fitzpatrick walked in. Today he wore a soft white polo shirt and jeans. Many of the female eyes in the restaurant shifted from me to him. I suddenly felt silly standing up in front of the ladies discussing whether or not to put your athletic shoes out to dry in direct sunlight.

Leo Fitzpatrick had a newspaper folded under his arm. He slid into a booth, and Jackie brought him a menu. He opened and glanced at it, but then he gazed across the table at me as I expounded on the virtues of cotton canvas.

The ladies clapped politely as I finished, and I started signing their copies of my book. As I put away my laptop, I was planning my exit. I grabbed my purse, slung it over my shoulder, turned abruptly and ran into Mr. Fitzpatrick, who was blocking my path. I jumped back and let out a short, high-pitched squeal.

"Sorry, I didn't mean to scare you or anything."

"That's okay," I gasped. I returned to gathering my things.

"I was wondering if you had eaten your lunch yet."

"My lunch?"

"Yes, your lunch. We are at a restaurant, and well, one of the drawbacks to being new in town is you don't have anyone to share a burger with."

Was he asking me to have lunch with him? It had been so long since a man asked me anything, that I wasn't sure if this was an invitation or just a statement of fact. Did I really want to do this? There was something about this guy I couldn't quite put my finger on. I knew, for Zach's sake, it wouldn't hurt to get to know the dad of the kid who was picking on him. There was also the little issue of getting his phone number for my dad. I relented. "As a matter of fact, I haven't eaten yet. I guess I could serve as the Pecan Bayou welcome wagon for you today."

"Of course, if you're too busy finding bodies ..." he joked.

"No, I think I'm at my limit for those."

We walked over to his table facing the front window. I slid into the red vinyl booth, parking my bag at the end. He slid in on the other side.

Jackie came over and smiled at me with the look of one fisherman to another, reeling one in. She snapped her gum and straightened a strand of freshly dyed red hair.

"Well, who is this, Betsy? You got a boyfriend now?"

"No, Mr. Fitzpatrick just moved here. His son and Zach are in the same scout troop."

"Uh huh." She wasn't buying my explanation, or maybe she was sizing him up for herself. "Well let me welcome you to Pecan Bayou, Mr. Fitzpatrick. What'll you have?" Jackie took our orders and flashed me a quick smile before heading off to the kitchen.

Now alone, I began to feel a little uncomfortable. I struggled to find something to say.

"So what exactly is it that you do?" Fitzpatrick asked as he unfolded his napkin.

"I give helpful hints to people. I blog. I write the 'Happy Hinter' column for the newspaper, I have a book, and I even started doing some business consulting."

"And that pays money?"

That was a little rude. "Yes," I replied. I get more steady paychecks than you investor types get, I thought, wondering if he was just another Barry.

I continued. "My father wanted me to get your number to ask you some questions about meeting Canfield at the old hospital."

One of the ladies from my presentation came over and placed a copy of my book in front of me.

"Miss Livingston. Thank you so much for speaking with us today. Would you sign this for me?"

"Sure." I grabbed her pen and started signing my name.

"Is this your husband? Nice to meet you." She extended a blue-veined hand out to Fitzpatrick.

"Uh, nice to meet you but I'm not ..."

The older woman picked up her book from the table. "Have fun, you two!" She giggled and scooted across the room.

"Man, this town really wants you to have a man in your life."

"Lucky me," I said with a quick smile and a shrug of my shoulders.

"I hope you're not too embarrassed," he said.

"No, it's quite a compliment compared to what they usually say about me."

Jackie returned with our burgers and placed them on the table. "Whatcha going to be for Halloween, Betsy?"

"A paranormal investigator, and you?" I asked.

"I'm torn between a prison matron or a sexy Little Red Riding Hood." She snapped her gum and smiled directly at Mr. Fitzpatrick. She angled slightly and put her hand on her hip. "Enjoy," she said, turning and swinging her hips seductively on her way back to the kitchen.

"I think she likes you," I told Fitzpatrick.

"She might change her mind when she finds out I've now have the opportunity to meet your father. He must quite proud of you. I'll bet he thought that right before he put me on the suspect list. I was walking around the old hospital, and I ran into Canfield. That's all there is to it."

I wasn't sure if Fitzpatrick was simply in the wrong place at the wrong time or if there was much more to this handsome stranger from Dallas. He did just arrive in town and within two weeks, Oliver Canfield was found dead.

"So tell me about this investor you've come to town for. Is it a big firm?"

"No, I wouldn't necessarily say big. I'm here for someone whose ... interests I'm protecting."

That was puzzling. Had his investor already put money into the old hospital?

"It's a private matter." He continued shutting down my next question.

"Okay." I played with a French fry. What was he hiding? Was his investor so hush-hush because he or she intended to put something up the town wouldn't like? What could it be? A prison? A landfill? It couldn't be good if he was clamming up this fast. Whatever was going on, hopefully my dad was on to it and would fill me in.

"By the way," said Fitzpatrick. "I wanted to let you know that Benny has put our boys together as buddies for the campout."

"Really?"

"Really," he confirmed.

Great, now Zach would have to spend the night with a kid who will probably use him for a punching bag. If it wasn't scheduled on Halloween, my dad could have gone along to watch out for him. I felt as if Zach was being thrown to the wolves. I had to find a way to make peace between the two boys.

"Unless we want to be pulling them apart as they battle all night, it might be a nifty idea to have a play date ahead of time," I suggested.

"A play date?" He acted as if he had never heard of the concept. How could he have a son as old as Tyler and not know what a play date was?

"Yes, you know. We get together, and the boys run off and hang out for a little while? Your wife really did cut you out of all the parent stuff, didn't she?"

"Oh ... that kind of play date." He nodded. "Sure. Would you like to take the boys to get hamburgers or something?"

Tyler was a pretty hefty guy, and I couldn't imagine he would have too much fun crawling around the colorful playground tubes and tunnels they had at our neighborhood fast food joint. Somehow I don't think Mr. Fitzpatrick had thought about it one way or another.

"That sounds good, but how about the two you come over to our house and eat supper? I make a pretty mean plate of spaghetti. After dinner, the boys can run off and play video games."

"Sure. That sounds great. It's really nice of you to have us over. Maybe we can get our boys to stop fighting. I really think Tyler would benefit from having a friend – and so would I." He smiled, showing straight white teeth, not unlike the wolf at Grandma's door.

CHAPTER EIGHT

TRYING NOT TO THINK about my unplanned lunch date, I sat in my kitchen an hour later working on newspaper columns for November. There were plenty of tips to share for planning a successful Thanksgiving dinner. I had begun my exhaustive search for the best turkey leftover recipe I could find. I always made a turkey for Zach and my dad, and it seemed we were eating leftovers for a couple of weeks. Why was turkey that dish that you couldn't wait to taste on Thanksgiving and then couldn't stand the sight of by the time December rolled around? That is probably the sole reason why so many people cook a ham at Christmastime.

A quiet rain tapped gently on the windows of my house, making even my air-conditioned room feel cozy. Maybe this was the beginning of a cool-down. I looked out the window at the increasing cloud line along the horizon. Was that an average October rain, or could we truly be getting an exceptionally late hurricane? Maybe tomorrow morning I would walk outside to take Zach to school and feel a refreshing breeze. I couldn't remember the last time I put on a sweater, except while shopping in the frozen foods section of the grocery store. I dreamed of feeling a chilly breeze caressing my skin – then it hit me. I *had* felt cool recently ... in the dead tunnel. The cold hit me from the inside out.

I knew Maggie wanted to go back and find a ghost, but she would have to drag me in by the ear to get me to go with her. Let the real ghost hunters tackle that one. I opened the door and stepped out into the light sprinkle. I felt the hothouse effect almost immediately. Humidity in the rain – isn't that redundant? Not in Texas.

Maggie pulled up in her old Cadillac and jumped out, umbrella in hand. "What are you doing standing in the rain, child?" she asked as she skittered up the walk to the door.

"Wishing it was November ... and cool."

"Wishing won't bring it any faster." She stepped up to the porch and pulled down her umbrella. "Let's go in – I've got news." I obediently followed Maggie into the house, the glass storm door slamming behind me.

"What's up?" I asked as Maggie removed her rain bonnet. Today's model was pink with tiny white poodles sprinkled artfully about it. She poured herself a cup of coffee from my coffee pot.

"What's up is that woman we knocked heads with at the old hospital. She's organizing a picket-line march against the television station right now. She stuck her head in all the stores downtown and told people a terrible thing was about to take place if they didn't come and stop it." Maggie pushed up her thick glasses.

"Great. I'm sure she's slamming your paranormal group every chance she gets," I said.

"Yes, well, I was down making a deposit at the bank, talking to Delores the teller, when Miss Boyle came in saying she had an announcement. I thought she was robbing the place. She started talking trash about our paranormal team and then told everybody it was going to be on NUTV for the world to see. She made it sound like a virus infecting the town. People were folding up their checkbooks and following Miss Boyle right out the door. Luckily, I don't think she saw me, or she would have torn into me right there on the spot."

"What is it with this woman?" I said as I watched my aunt knock back her coffee and plunk the mug on the counter. I clicked off my computer.

"Let me get my umbrella." I walked over to the hall closet and pulled out my polka-dot umbrella. It fit there nicely now that the golf clubs were gone. "Do you think there's a chance she could really get the station shut down?"

"If she keeps riling up the public like this, who knows? I just know somebody needs to counter this trash she's spreading around."

"Let's call the station on the way. They can do a special report and then put our side of the story on the air as well."

"With a crowd gathering outside, I'll bet they have a clue something's wrong, don't ya think? Besides, Howard is already down there. He called me while I was driving over here." Maggie started pulling her plastic hair bonnet back on and tying the skinny plastic ties under her chin.

"It's tough enough for NUTV that most people around here are watching the Houston or Dallas stations where they can get all the network programming," I said, not bothering to put a raincoat on. I had a choice between getting a little damp or very hot, and figured I could put up with a little water. We slogged to her car and jumped in. Maggie drove while I called directory assistance and got the number for the station. The rain was pounding down on the windows, making Maggie's old windshield wipers wheeze with the torrent.

"I don't think she'll get too much of a crowd in this!" I shouted over the downpour.

"Yeah ... well ... we can only hope," Maggie said.

THE RAIN WAS COMING down harder as we pulled up to the NUTV station, which was housed in an historic two-story building at the end of Main Street. It had once been a hardware store with an apartment on the second floor. Every time I looked at it, I guessed the fancy gingerbread window cupolas were the hardware store owner's attempt to appease his wife and add a little class to their apartment over the store.

The lower half of the building consisted of a wood front that needed a new coat of paint. The front door, flanked by two small windows, was weathered wood with an NUTV sign nailed to it. Just in case the townspeople of Pecan Bayou missed the first sign, there was another sign to the side of the building made from a slice of the hanging tree that was cut down in the '60s. In old Texas, the hanging tree was always close to the courthouse. One-stop justice.

Miss Boyle stood on the narrow sidewalk in front of the station, dressed in a yellow slicker and holding a sign that read "Get the NUTS off of NUTV!" Behind her, peering out through the wooden blinds of the station, I could see Howard and the station manager, Stanley Gibson, watching Miss Boyle's antics. I wasn't sure if Howard wasn't coming out because it was raining or because, of all the apparitions and spirits he'd seen in his ghost hunting experiences, Miss Boyle was the thing that truly scared him. A small gathering of concerned citizens, sheltered beneath their umbrellas, blocked our entrance to the station door. I mentally noted that none of the ladies from the Best Little Hair House were in attendance. They were probably the wrong crowd to ask to go out in the rain, no matter what the cause.

We parked across the street, and as I got out of the car, popping up my umbrella, I could hear Maureen Boyle shouting over the driving pellets of moisture.

"Do you want the devil setting up shop in our town?"

The crowd responded with a weak "No."

It was almost as if they were being affronted by evil itself at the door and were still pulling on their house slippers. "*Oh, the devil's here ... um ... just one minute, let me get that porch light on for ya.*"

Maureen Boyle went on with her diatribe as we came to the edge of the crowd. "Mr. Oliver Canfield, a beloved citizen of this town, has now died out there. He was out there trying to make our town a better place, and this is what he got for it. He couldn't have known the type of people who frequent an abandoned structure like that. He has died, as countless others have out in that forlorn place. God rest the souls of these people. Someone has to preserve their dignity. Is our local television station NUTV helping to do just that? The answer is no. They are putting on a so-called paranormal circus out there tromping over the graves of our loved ones. These people have no heart, no compassion and no regard for our little town. They are bogeymen themselves – the living kind."

Maggie started pushing through the crowd. "That's it!" she piped, in her small voice. "That's it." She elbowed her way to the sidewalk. As the crowd moved out of the way for her, I had no choice but to follow my aunt. Aunt Maggie turned to the crowd. She was so short they could barely see her, so grabbing my hand, she hoisted herself up on a concrete planter in front of the building.

"I represent the Pecan Bayou Paranormal Society, and I am here to say that we do not nor have we ever participated in devil worship."

"Do not believe her," Maureen Boyle interrupted. "She speaks with the forked tongue of the devil's handmaiden. What would Oliver Canfield say if he could speak up right now? What would he tell us about her?"

Maggie ignored her. "We're a group of investigators who get together to examine claims of paranormal activity. We want to discover and record credible evidence of potential paranormal activity through audio and video devices. Everything we collect we want to connect to provable science."

"Bunk!" Miss Boyle replied. "You are opening Satan's doors to let out his host of evildoers."

I looked at the fear in Miss Boyle's eyes. She was a woman with a whole lot of demons right there inside her head. What terrified her so much about Maggie trying to find ghosts?

"Yes, well ..." Miss Boyle droned on, the yellow plastic of her slicker rattling with each gesture. "At the next meeting of the town council, I will tell you how we will take action against these invaders of the common good."

Maggie put her hands on her hips in defiance. "And the town council just can't wait to listen to all this tripe you're sputterin.'"

Miss Boyle turned slowly toward Maggie, pure hatred in her gaze. Her voice, which had been going into a higher register as she addressed the crowd, had now become low and directed at my aunt.

"Once the council hears what I have to say, you can bet your little ghost hunting adventure will be over." She turned back to the crowd, raising her voice again. "I am passing around this petition for all of you to sign to stop the Halloween broadcast. Please do what you feel is right and sign it. I will present the petition to the town council tonight."

"What can they do?" Aunt Maggie asked me. "They don't make the laws around here."

"Even though we have permission from the police, there might be a possibility the town council could put a stop to the investigation. That old hospital is owned by the town," I said.

During Miss Boyle's speech, several members of the crowd left. She now made her way around to the few people left out in the rain and shoved the soggy paper toward them. Some of the people shook their heads and started off down the street, seeming to use their umbrellas as shields against her angry tirade. Crazy Elmer Simms smiled at her with his one craggy tooth and gleefully signed his name.

Maggie and I escaped from the thinning crowd and protestations of Miss Boyle, and stepped into the offices of NUTV.

Our little cable access channel was owned by Martin and Sally Gibson. It was partially financed by the town council and ran local events like Friday night high school football games, which doubled as religious services for some of the Pecan Bayou residents. NUTV also televised Miss Melody's School of Dance recitals, a live broadcast from the chili cook-off and set up a camera in the second story of Neuman's store to film the various parades throughout the year. The station manager was Stanley Gibson, the only son of the owners. He was in his thirties with an affection for argyle sweater vests and bow ties. He had never married, which didn't seem to be much of a surprise to the town, what with his love for his show tune music collection.

Stanley turned from where he had been standing in the front office, peeking at the crowd through the wooden blinds.

"Welcome, Maggie. I'm glad you made your way through the crowd."

Howard looked out of the other window, still watching the demonstration. Today he was wearing a western vest, bolo tie, denim shorts and cowboy boots. Who dressed this guy?

Stan continued. "It seems we are the talk of the town right now. I was on the phone this morning with my parents, and it seems Ms. Boyle has stated that she will make sure we lose the town council's support for all of our programming if we don't stay away from the hospital."

Miss Boyle had attacked on yet another front. Her onslaught of attacks made me wonder if maybe there was gold under that there dead tunnel.

Stanley walked around to his desk and pulled out a ledger. He ran his hand along a column. "Look, I can see that the Pecan Bayou Paranormal Society has already paid the fee to use the film crew that night, but there is a possibility we may have to refund your money. We are happy to produce your show but not at the price of losing the station."

"It seems to me that if the police could figure out who killed Oliver Canfield, a lot of this would die down," I said, watching the last of the crowd get in their cars.

Maggie crossed her arms and rolled her eyes.

"That would be nice dear," she said. "You know, Stan, we really are doing a paranormal investigation. It is not any form of devil worship or voodoo or whatever she's callin' it. Why can't she make that distinction?"

"She's a nonbeliever of the worst sort." Howard turned from the window. "Not only doesn't she believe, but the mere possibility of another world existing terrifies her."

"And because to her everything is black or white," Stan added. "You're either in league with the devil or the angels."

Stan pushed his chair into the desk and put his hands upright on the blotter, as if praying. "Whatever she's afraid of, it poses a risk to our little station. Very few towns agree to put out the funds to sponsor their own television station. I would hate to lose their support."

"If we can figure out why Canfield was killed, then maybe Miss Boyle will lighten up," I said. Finding out more about Canfield wouldn't hurt my situation either.

Maggie put her hand on her shoulder. "Betsy, even if you solve a hundred murders, it will not change the fact that we are doing something Miss Boyle doesn't approve of."

"I just want to know why she was wandering around in the weeds at the hospital the other day. Was she just driving around and happened to see us over there? What's her story?" I asked.

Stan straightened his bow tie. "Maybe she heard you were doing your investigation and it so incensed her, she showed up to stop you."

"Howard," I said, "how many people knew we were doing a preliminary walk-through on Wednesday?"

"As far as I know, it was just the three of us," he answered.

"Maybe we need to ask her at the town council meeting just exactly what she was doing there. When my dad asked her, she just stomped off."

Stan's brow wrinkled, and he shook his head. "Well, whatever you do, don't get her so angry she shuts down the station."

"First of all, she has to find someone who actually is bothered by the investigation," said Maggie. "From what I can tell, she hasn't come up with anybody yet. I don't even know anyone from the town who had a friend or relative die out there, come to think of it."

It was kind of funny, but neither did I. Maybe Miss Boyle lost somebody out there? She was older than I was but by no means old. Miss Boyle was almost as much of a mystery as Oliver Canfield's murder.

CHAPTER NINE

LATER THAT EVENING, as Maggie, Zach, Danny and I entered the maple-paneled town council room, I could see the three council members sitting up at the dais. Two of the men I recognized as the Schuller brothers, Tom and Don. Tom ran Schuller Auto, while Don was in charge of the local chamber of commerce. They were both in their late forties and looked just alike except for the fact that even though both were bald, Tom had a full head of hair. Not exactly the hair God gave him, but he looked pretty dapper. The two of them often voted together on the council, which gave them a monopoly on how the town was run. It was a terrific deal for them, but when they disagreed, which wasn't often, the whole city would know about it. We thought there would be bloodshed on the trash pick-up issue.

The third man on the council was our own Dr. MacPhee. He looked smaller up there next to the two burly Schuller men. He wore a maroon vest and tie, and smiled out at his wife Lillian, who was sitting in the front row. She had silver hair coiffed neatly so as to complement her muted navy ruffled blouse and matching slacks. It was clear she didn't shop at the SuperWally sale rack.

Lillian MacPhee was a member of the Piper's Hills Country Club set and a true style leader in this town. I glanced down at my faded leather sandals worn under my denim capris and tried to straighten out the hem of my soft blue plaid shirt. Quite a contrast.

Leo Fitzpatrick entered with his son Tyler. Tyler immediately went over to a chair, slumped into it and pulled out a handheld video game. Zach was working on adding sums in his chair. I glanced over to him with pride, thinking what a good parent I was and then noticed some lovely stick people all over his homework paper. Fitzpatrick sat next to his sullen son and folded his arms across his chest. He had to be the best-looking man to hit this town in a while, but he didn't seem to be the kind of guy who knew it. His eyes rose from his son's game and immediately zeroed in on me. I quickly averted my gaze to another direction. Busted.

"The meeting will come to order," said Tom Schuller, tapping a gavel on the dais.

"We have been called to this emergency town council meeting in order to address an issue that has come to our attention this week. Miss Maureen Boyle has the floor."

Miss Boyle quickly rose, her notes clutched to her small bosom, and walked to the podium in front of the dais. She adjusted the microphone up a bit to accommodate her height, cleared her voice, and began.

"Thank you, Councilman Schuller." She forced a smile and aimed it at each member of the council. "I come to you this evening because of a spiritual abomination about to occur at the Johnson Tuberculosis Hospital. The structure itself has been closed off to the public for years, but now the local police have decided to give a group of so-called paranormal worshipers free rein over its rooms full of sad, sad history. I should also add that the police have admitted they have relatives in this group and will fully support them no matter what they do."

I could feel Maggie starting to wiggle next to me. She was ready to jump up and defend herself. She would be given a chance to speak after Miss Boyle finished assassinating the character of the Pecan Bayou Paranormal Society.

"It is because of this that I ask the council to consider banning this fringe group and all others from the site and that the council discourage any kind of filming by our local station. The broadcast of this program could warp our young people for God knows how long. It is a disgrace that our station would even consider this type of program to be broadcast right here in our homes. Quite possibly, this brings into question the town's financial support of NUTV and the programming they are accepting for payment."

"Yes, yes," said Don Schuller. "I can understand your discomfort with the situation, Miss Boyle. Did I come to understand there was some sort of police investigation going on out there at present?"

"That is exactly right, sir. It seems there was foul play out at the old hospital, and one of our citizens was murdered. Now this group of ... vultures ..." Her eyes scanned the crowd and lit upon Maggie. "...want to raise the spirits of the dead. Including the spirit of the murdered man, Oliver Canfield, one of the town's most prominent businessmen."

The crowd murmured on that last statement. Canfield's reputation preceded him, so the prominent businessman part probably wasn't settling in too well. "This is a group and an event in our community we do not have to condone, gentlemen," she said to the council, "and we look to your leadership to rid us of these satanic influences."

Howard bolted up in the back of the room. It seemed he had finally scrounged up enough courage to confront Miss Boyle. His eyes bugged out as the anger rose to his face. "That is not true!"

Tom Schuller pounded his gavel. "Miss Boyle has the floor, sir."

I felt Maggie jump up beside me. "She sure does, because I wouldn't step on the garbage she's throwin' out. We are not affiliated with anything Satanic. I'm sitting in the pew same as you each week. I just don't lord it over others as you are apt to do."

Tom Schuller banged the gavel again. "Order!"

Miss Boyle's mouth soured. "As you can see, members of the council, these are the kinds of people we are forced to deal with in this situation."

"And what kind of people is that, you ... you ..." Maggie responded.

Tom Schuller interrupted before my aunt could fill in the blank. "If you would like to speak, Mrs. Schaeffer, then stand behind Miss Boyle at the podium and wait your turn."

Maggie left the seating area, heaved an indignant sigh and took her place behind Miss Boyle. The two of them were a contrast in height standing next to each other. My aunt's head was right about at Miss Boyle's bony shoulder blades. Miss Boyle turned slightly, looked down her nose directly at her and continued.

"I would like to move that all access to the hospital be prohibited to the Pecan Bayou Paranormal Society on Halloween or any other day."

Miss Boyle gathered herself and glowered at my aunt as she left the podium.

When it was her turn to speak, Maggie reached up to adjust the microphone but could not quite get her fingertips on the top. Howard hastened to the front to help her out with the mic. After making the adjustment, he took up a position next to her. It was the bravest thing I had seen him do in our short association.

"Gentlemen," she started quietly. It was a distinct contrast to the near-yelling she had focused on Miss Boyle a few moments earlier. Aunt Maggie was pulling on every ounce of reserve she had to follow the decorum of the town council. "The Pecan Bayou Paranormal Society is not an agent of the devil. We are people who are curious, that's all. We're curious about the possibility of an existence on another plane. I lost my husband, Jeeter, a few years back, and for a while there I didn't think I could go on. One of the comforts I have found is in my faith, that's true. But until I get there and meet him on that celestial cloud, I would just love to know where he is and if he's all right. Sounds crazy, I know. And I know I'm not going to find him floatin' around out there at the hospital."

"What about the argument that the site is unsafe?" asked Don Schuller.

Howard lowered his head to speak into the microphone. "Sir, we have done a preliminary safety check of the property and have found the structure still very solid."

Arvin Wilson, Chief of Police, stood up in the back of the room. He had on the same navy blue uniform my dad wore with a few extra pieces of brass affixed. He pushed his glasses up his nose with one finger, and stepped forward. "If I may add, Don. My men have checked through the site, and there has been an officer posted there at the crime scene ever since the discovery of Mr. Canfield. We want to find who killed Mr. Canfield and need to protect the crime scene. Lieutenant Kelsey has spoken in depth with the members of the paranormal group and made sure they know what they can and cannot do. With all of these conditions in place, I think the coexistence of the police and ghost hunters will be fine." He stepped back and tipped his Stetson, making me think of a knight stepping away from a king.

Leo Fitzpatrick, who had been listening quietly, rose from his chair and raised his hand.

"Yes, sir," said Tom Schuller. "If you have something to present to the council, please come to the podium so everyone can hear you."

Fitzpatrick strode to the front of the meeting room. "My name is Leo Fitzpatrick, and I just wanted to ask what kind of plans the town has for the old hospital."

Don Schuller leaned back in his well-padded chair. "Can't say we have much of a plan at present, Mr. Fitzpatrick."

Dr. MacPhee added, "That old place has been there for so long, most of us have forgotten about it."

"So there was no plan in place to develop it?"

"Not that I know of. Nothing has come through the chamber of commerce," Don said.

"Thank you." Fitzpatrick left the podium.

"Well you've certainly all given us something to think about," said Tom Schuller. "The investigation is scheduled to be completed on Saturday, Halloween, and it is now Thursday night. We will take about twenty-four hours to discuss, research and come to our decision. I would like to schedule another meeting tomorrow afternoon, if that is okay with the other members of the council?" He looked at his brother and Dr. MacPhee.

The other two nodded in agreement.

"See you all tomorrow, then." The crowd rose from their chairs and began filing from the room. Leo Fitzpatrick stood with his son and glanced back at our little group. Fitzpatrick smiled and raised his hand with an awkward wave. As I waved back, I caught his son sneering at mine. I turned to Zach and blocked his view of Tyler.

"Mom?" Zach said. "Were they talking about the place where you found Da – Mr. Canfield?"

"Yes," I said.

"Very sad," bemoaned Danny as he folded his hands in front and shook his head.

"Could I go with you on Halloween and see where you found him?" Zach said.

Here's an issue you don't find in the parenting magazines – do you take your child to a crime scene or not? I looked down at Zach, who was putting his schoolwork back into his bag, his eyes pleading with mine, a little smile playing on his lips.

"Come on Mom, I would stay out of your way."

"No," I told him.

"You wouldn't even know I was there. Besides, I could help carry in equipment. Right, Aunt Maggie?"

Maggie just shook her head no. Zach had hit a tough crowd.

"I'm going," said Danny.

Zach's eyes grew wider in disbelief. "You're letting Danny go but not me? That's not fair."

We walked out the door to the parking lot. "Danny's going because I can't leave him alone overnight, and all of us are over there. I need him with me. He's going to be up for a while and then sleep on a cot next to the NUTV van," Maggie said.

"You could put up two cots!" Zach said.

"Cool," said Danny. "It'll be a sleepover!"

"Did you forget you already have an obligation that evening?" I said. "You will only be across the field in the woods camping with the Scouts. If anything big happens, I'll let you know, okay?" Zach looked at the ground sulking. I repeated, "Okay?"

"Okay," he muttered.

CHAPTER TEN

ZACH CONTINUED TO SULK as we walked. I glanced at my watch. It was nearly eight o'clock, and it was getting close to Zach's bedtime. Thinking of my schedule for the next few days, I figured we would need to make one more stop before going home. We walked to the back door of the courthouse where the parking lot was.

"So Zach," I said, changing the subject. "How about you and I go down to SuperWally and look for a costume for you for the campout?"

He uncrossed his arms and smiled slowly. "That would be cool," he said, his voice raising a note with each word. He loved going to the local superstore, and he loved Halloween shopping, so the argument over the abandoned hospital vanished.

"I know just what I want to be – an axe murderer."

"No."

"Mo-om," Zach intoned as if a dying tea kettle, "why not?"

"First of all, it's too violent. You will be out there with little kids, and you could scare one of them."

Aunt Maggie, who, with Danny by her side, had been following us, added, "Zachary, do you really want to go through the whole night with sticky red stuff all over?"

"Yuck," grimaced Danny.

Zach droned on. "Mo-om, it's Halloween. You think they're going to see little fluffy blue bears all night?"

We came to the large glass doors and pushed them open into the muggy night.

"I don't know, but you don't have to add to the scary stuff they will see," I said.

"How about you go as one of them super heroes?" Aunt Maggie said.

"I don't look good in tights." Zach folded his arms back across his chest in frustration. I hated seeing him do that, because it was a mannerism Barry had been particularly fond of. How could he learn that gesture if he hadn't ever met him?

"Okay, how about going as something from a video game?" I asked.

Zach nodded his head slowly in interest with this new idea. "Hmmm, maybe I could go as ... a zombie."

"Oh dear, I guess we're parked on the other side, dearie," my aunt said. "Get your rest and don't be too late picking out just the right getup."

"Bye Betsy. Bye Zach," Danny said. We waved and walked on alone. In an effort to save the town money, the new mayor had deemed the parking lot lights be turned off at 8 p.m. The moonlight shed a weak illumination on the trees and bushes.

"So what do you think of the zombie idea?" Zach continued as we walked in the blackness. A bush to the side stirred. I tried to focus into it through the darkness. The light was too dim for me to see if there was a person next to the bush. This whole paranormal business had me looking at anything that moved in the shadows. Zach had stopped waiting for me to answer. He continued making what he thought was an exceptional bargain.

"They only have a little blood, you know, if they've just eaten someone's brains or something," he said, as if to assure me.

"Yeah, yeah," I said and shrugged. I had seen *Night of the Living Dead* as a kid and couldn't get it out of my head for weeks.

"So can I be a zombie? Please?" Zach put his hands together as if to beg for the last morsel of bread on the planet.

"I'll think about it." I honestly didn't have a strong enough reason to tell him no, but a zombie?

I had pulled into a space that skirted a bank of trees next to the parking lot. As we approached it, I could see our headlights dimly lighting the shadowy trunks.

"Oh no," I said. Had I actually done this? Had I left my lights on?

"What's wrong, Mom?"

I ran to the car, unlocked the door and hopped in. I put the key in the ignition and turned it, only to be greeted with the unwelcome sound of a dying starter.

Zach listened. "Mom, our car sounds sick. Try turning the key harder."

"And when was it that you got that certificate in automobile mechanics?"

"Sorry," he replied. He waited while I turned the key harder, to no avail. His mind still on the costume, Zach went on with our former conversation.

"Okay, here's another idea for Halloween."

"And what would that be?" I asked, sucking in my breath.

"Get this," he said. "I want to be a mad scientist."

I tried the key one more time, only to be greeted with the same noise, just a little weaker this time. "A mad scientist? That's it? Well that's doable."

I looked around the parking lot to see if other people were heading out to their cars. It seemed everyone had parked in the front this evening. I wondered if the shadow in the bushes had any jumper cables. I started calculating how late SuperWally would be open if I had to call a tow truck. Too bad I didn't have a hint in my book for starting a car with a drained battery.

"Of course we'll need to find a chainsaw and some fake blood," Zach continued.

"Excuse me? Did you say a chainsaw? This is starting to sound surprisingly similar to the axe murderer idea."

"Uh, he is a MAD scientist after all."

"Couldn't you just carry a test tube around or something? A chainsaw can get pretty heavy, you know."

"Mom! Not a real chainsaw!" He looked at me in shock. "I could hurt myself. I am a kid, you know. I mean a toy one. You can get one at the store with blood painted on it."

What has our society come to when a child could go to a store and pick up a bloody chainsaw toy? "I see. What about a white lab coat? Can I get one of those there as well?"

"Nah. The only kinds of costumes they have are princesses and comic book guys." Zach sighed and tapped his chin with his finger. "Maybe ... we could ask Grandpa's friend, Mr. Rivera. He is a coroner, after all. I'm sure he must have some mad scientist stuff somewhere."

Knowing Art, he would probably say yes to the request. I just hoped he didn't give Zach any real blood to put on the chainsaw.

"You think you could ask him if he has one?" Zach asked.

"Sure," I answered.

It was then I finally accepted my car was dead.

"I think we're stuck."

"Call Grandpa," Zach said.

"Zach, I can survive one day without calling Grandpa."

"Call Grandpa."

I grumbled and then pulled out my cell phone and dialed my dad's number. After just a few admonishments, my dad told me that he was on his way out the door. Barry's old car had died, even though I turned the key harder.

Zach and I waited there, sitting in the darkened car. Zach pushed a little button on the side of his Scout watch to illuminate it. It was around 8:15. If my dad got here in the next few minutes, we would still have time to look around for a costume at SuperWally. I looked out at the shadows playing amid the bushes. A slight breeze ruffled the branches. Finally, I spotted the lights of my dad's cruiser as he pulled into the parking lot.

I popped the hood as he exited his car with the jumper cables.

"So you left your lights on?" he said, not feeling the need to start with the customary greeting of "hello."

"Uh, yeah, I really appreciate you coming out to help."

"Where else would I be when my daughter and grandson need my help?" Zach crawled out of his side of the car and tapped on my shoulder.

"Is this a good time to tell you I promised the Scouts that you would bring some of your homemade cookies to the campout?"

I could not express in words how much this wasn't a good time to tell me this. "You promised and then forgot? Oh, Zach."

"Please, Mom. All the kids are depending on me. I told them that you bake great cookies. You can do it. You have time. Please?"

"Ugh. I don't know, Zach. I'll have to work on them tonight."

"Thanks, Mom! You're the best."

"Yep, that's me."

My dad chuckled. "Sweetheart, did I ever tell you how nice it is to see all of the junk you did to me as a parent coming back to zing you with Zach?"

I rolled my eyes. "Glad to make life so sweet for you, Dad."

Zach climbed into the back seat of the cruiser and started bouncing up and down. Anyone driving by might have guessed my dad had just arrested the town's most notorious kangaroo.

"Grandpa, are you taking us to get a costume? Are you?" Zach yelled from the backseat.

My dad raised his eyebrows, wondering what I had just gotten him into. "I hadn't planned on it, sport."

"Mom and I were going to SuperWally to get me a costume. I need it for the campout this weekend."

"A costume at a campout? I don't know if that's a good idea."

"It gets worse. He wants to go as something scary like a guy with an axe."

My dad scowled. "Why would you want to go as one of the bad guys, Zach? How about you get on the right side of the law? Would you like to be a junior deputy for the one and only Pecan Bayou Police Department?"

Zach's eyes widened. "I could do that?"

"Well, we don't bestow that honor on just anyone, mind you, but I know your upstanding character, and I can speak for you, so the answer is yes."

"Cool!" He bounced even more.

My dad looked around from under the hood of my car. "Okay, sweetheart. Try it."

I pressed on the gas pedal and heard the car come to life again.

"You're going to need to replace that battery, Betsy," my father said as he disconnected the cables from the positive and negative ports of the batteries. "What do you say Zach comes home with me and we'll look at some of my old uniforms?"

"Thanks, Grandpa! That would be excellent!"

"Thanks, Dad," I echoed.

"And then maybe we could spill a little fake blood on the front," Zach said softly, almost to himself.

"NO!" My dad and I both answered in unison.

"Tell you what. I'll take Zach over to my house, find an old uniform for him, and he can just spend the night. That way you can dedicate all of your time to making those delicious cookies."

"Thanks, Dad." I reached across to hug his shoulder, and he turned and smiled.

"That is, if you save a few for me."

"Deal."

CHAPTER ELEVEN

I KNEW I NEEDED EGGS if I was going to be baking all night, so I stopped off at the Best Buys Grocery Store. As I pulled in to park, I noticed that Zach had left part of his math homework in the passenger side, and it looked as if it was about to slide under the seat. I turned off the car and reached down to attempt to pull out the paper, which had become wedged under the seat. I reached my hand farther under the seat to dislodge it, a little worried what else I might find. I tried to grab for the paper but came up with something lumpy and metal instead. At last, I found the corner of the paper and slid it out.

Curious about the metal lump, I slid my hand back under the seat and tried pulling out the small object. I could feel the familiar metal ridges of keys. I couldn't remember the last time I had lost my keys. I had always been pretty responsible about hanging my keys on a peg in the kitchen. Barry, on the other hand, had misplaced his keys at least once a week, and I know we had to replace them at least once during our short marriage. The one time I teased him about it, he blew up at me and told me to quit nagging him. I remember how being surprised at how sensitive he became at the slightest criticism. Reaching around the back end of the seat, I pulled out the long-forgotten keys. I held them up to the light shining from the post of the grocery store parking lot.

The ring held several keys and a keychain ornament with a Canfield Investments logo on it. Could this be an old set of Barry's keys? How long had they been down there? There were only a couple of keys on the ring, so they were probably his office keys. They had been wedged under the seat, which explains why my car vacuuming had missed them.

I remembered his old office in the bank building downtown. I brought in some plants to help with the decorating when he first moved in, but only visited a few times after that. Barry would always put off my suggestions to come downtown for lunch. He told me that he preferred to be all business at work, and then he added, almost as an afterthought, that I would be too much of a distraction for him. Now I knew he just didn't want me finding out about whatever it was he and Canfield were doing. If Canfield had returned to that office when he came back to Pecan Bayou, I wondered if the keys would still work. I also wondered how he was paying the rent without a partner to split the cost. I hadn't seen any real estate signs with Canfield's name on them around town.

After Barry disappeared, Oliver Canfield did come by the house one time to bring a box of Barry's things. He sat on the edge of our old couch and told me if I needed anything just to call him. It probably would have sounded like a legitimate offer if he hadn't been out my front door within the next two minutes.

I thought of Barry as I held his keys in my hands once again. Keys that he had forgotten, that had stayed buried in this old car for the past seven years. I fingered the metal ridges.

I wondered if they would still work. No, I couldn't. I had to buy eggs and bake cookies. I stuffed the keys into my purse and headed for the grocery store.

As I stood at the checkout a few minutes later, I noticed all of the pregnant celebrities on the cover of the gossip magazines. Now, pregnant celebrities were delicately described as having a "baby bump." That way they could still be seen on the beach in their bikinis sporting a "bump" but still looking incredibly beautiful. I thought about Celia, who had much more than a "bump" to carry around. Even though she was much bigger than the starlets I saw pictured on the magazines, she was also just as beautiful, even if she couldn't get her wedding ring on anymore. I wondered if she thought to take it off before her hands got bigger or if she had to use butter to get her ring off. When I had been pregnant with Zach, I didn't know my hands would swell. I barely got my ring off in time. Canfield's hand came to my mind. Had he been trying to take a ring off just before he was shot? There were so many things I still needed to know.

"Did you find everything you needed?" the checkout girl asked.

"Just about," I answered. Just about.

I HELD BARRY'S KEYS in my hands as steered my car into the parking lot of the bank building. It wasn't as if I were going to the crime scene. I had been offered an opportunity to look inside Canfield's office and see just what he and probably Barry had been up to all those years ago. If my dad had been given this opportunity, he might have done the same thing, I rationalized.

I looked up at the town's oldest two-story building. It housed our bank, which was situated at the end of a two-floor atrium lined with smaller offices. I slipped into the main lobby door. The unmistakable odor of cleaning products lingered in the air, and I saw a cleaning cart outfitted with squirt bottles and a large trash bag holder. A woman looked down as she cleaned inside an accounting office. A strain of tinny portable radio music drifted across the open area.

Not wanting to take a chance she would look up, I waited until she turned her back to vacuum in an inner office. I darted across the lobby to the stairway leading to the second floor. My eyes shot to the accountant's door again, and I could hear a chorus of singers coming over the radio. Whoever was cleaning probably wouldn't hear me ascend the stairway. I took off up the stairs, got to the top and looked down again on the open lobby. The woman pushed the vacuum out of the back office and started emptying trash cans. I blended into the shadows on the unlit second floor.

I pulled out my keys and tried the lock. Whether I had the right keys for the lock became a moot point as I realized that the door was already unlocked. Maybe it had been opened for the cleaning lady. If so, I would need to make this a speedy search. I was in. Canfield's office looked as if it had been updated since Barry's days. My plants were gone and replaced by tasteful potted palms. There was a large oak desk next to a brown stone wall and a leather couch next to a large window. The wood floors shone and were tastefully covered with a brown and gold oriental rug.

Using what little light I had streaming in from the downstairs lobby, I started going through the items on Canfield's desk. There were no pictures of a wife, and if Canfield had any children, there was no trace of them. Reaching into the middle drawer, I found an appointment book. I leafed through the pages of the small book to see that he had spent the year in various deals around the state with appointments in Dallas and Fort Worth, as well as Pecan Bayou. On the Wednesday before his death, he had an appointment with Benny and one with someone named Bitsy. He also had a scheduled time next to a scrawled JTB, which I had to assume was the Johnson Tuberculosis Hospital. This appointment was with someone named Roy.

I knew who Benny was, but who the heck was Bitsy? I couldn't remember a soul in town named Roy. I searched further and found a sketch of what looked like a layout for a mall. That must have been his idea for the property. Pecan Bayou did not have a mall as of yet. Most people drove over to Andersonville to do their department-store shopping.

I searched through his right desk drawer. I found memo pads, business cards and a few scattered breath mints. My hand skimmed over something sticking up in the back. I tried to grasp it as all of Canfield's business cards came sliding toward me. I seemed to be lifting out the bottom of the drawer. I pulled it completely out, letting the cards and mints hit the floor. I had stumbled onto a hidden section in the drawer.

In this new hidden compartment, I found several credit cards and a couple of identification cards with Oliver Canfield's picture on them, but not his name. One read Javier Torres and another had the name Oscar Bianchi. It seemed Mr. Canfield, or whoever he was, had more than one identity. I looked at the credit cards and was surprised to see they were all issued to women. Ruby Morris, Martha Johnson, Molly Baumgartner and – I couldn't believe it – Maureen Boyle. What was he doing with her credit card? Did he steal it from her, or did she give it to him? If I hadn't just broken into this office, I would be calling my dad. Trying to explain how I learned this information was a conversation I didn't want to be having right now.

I looked for Canfield's computer. There was an empty area on his desk where it should have been. The police were probably searching through his hard drive as part of their investigation.

I turned around and headed toward a row of filing cabinets on the back wall. Upon opening the first drawer, I found files listed by property. It seemed Mr. Canfield closed more real estate deals than I had been aware of. In the next drawer, the files were listed by last name. Once again I saw some of the same names I had seen printed on the credit cards. I reached for the file marked "Maureen Boyle" when suddenly the reflection from the lobby lights went black. Upon turning around, I looked through to the glassed-in front office. The entire building was dark. Had there been a power outage? I walked forward a few steps and felt pain shoot up my leg as my knee collided with the corner of Canfield's desk. I placed my hands on the desk for leverage and tried to see the path to Canfield's office doorway. I heard a soft sound in the next room. Could that be the outer door opening? Had the cleaning lady come up here? I crouched down by the desk. If it was her, I couldn't let her see me. I could hear breathing as whoever it was moved around the room. I tried to hold my breath.

My phone jangled "The Eyes of Texas are Upon You." I jammed my hand into my pocket, trying to grab at it.

"Dad!" I whispered a scream. Then pain spread across my skull as something hard hit me in the back of the head.

I CAME TO WITH A SUDDEN jolt as I coughed to clear something in my chest. I coughed again, feeling pain as my lungs labored to breathe. Smoke was everywhere. My eyes fixed on a bright light now illuminating the doorway. Was the office on fire? Staying away from the clouds of smoke I saw billowing above me, I started crawling towards the door. My head throbbed, and I recognized the coppery taste of blood in my mouth. As I came close to the fire, I forced myself to stand up, although my head felt like a giant bell was ringing inside of it. I took a deep breath and immediately went into another cough for my efforts. I shut my eyes and leapt over a darting flame, ready to feel the impact of my body hitting the floor on the other side.

"Betsy!" The voice was familiar, but I couldn't make out the figure, other than it was a man. As he drew closer to me, I started backing towards the painful heat of the flames. Was this Canfield's killer? He edged in closer and grabbed me under the arms.

"It's okay, Betsy. It's me, Leo," he said gently. "We have to get out of here now." We hobbled together to the stairs. We were now overlooking more dancing flames edging toward us on the bottom floor.

"Can you get down the stairs?" he yelled over the thunder of the fire.

"I'll try," I said, as I tried to see my own feet on the floor. How was it that the place was on fire and spinning too?

I put both hands on the stair railing to find it was hot, so I held onto Fitzpatrick behind me. Together we started down the stairs, one by one. When we reached the bottom, we ran for the door.

The cleaning cart was now abandoned by the accountant's office. I wondered if the cleaning woman got out. I tried to tell Fitzpatrick about her but couldn't seem to speak very well. What if she was trapped in there? I could see the red-and-blue flash of the fire trucks and police department.

Running in from the street with Zachary in pajamas, I saw my father.

Zachary ran into my arms. "Mom!" was all he screamed before burying his head into my shoulder. Fitzpatrick stepped back. My dad, heaving the sigh of a father whose daughter couldn't seem to stay out of trouble, watched the building grow into a larger blaze. "Betsy, what the hell were you doing in there? I thought you were going to bake cookies!"

"I was," I confessed that I found an old set of Barry's keys. "I was in Canfield's office. I had to know."

"It was a damn fool idea. That's what it was. You could have been killed, do you know that? Now I'm thinkin' having that GPS gadget on your phone was the best idea you ever had."

"Mom," Zach joined his grandfather in scolding me, "you could have been killed. It was a ..."

"Okay, okay," I answered, holding my hand up to stop the two-generation lecture.

"Thank God Mr. Fitzpatrick pulled you out of the building."

I looked around behind us. I saw the cleaning lady now sitting on the curb with a paramedic putting a blanket around her.

"Where did he go?" I asked.

"I don't know," my father said, turning around in the parking lot in an effort to find him.

"That's strange," I said. "Why would he go running off like that?"

"And what the hell was he doing here in the first place?" said my dad.

CHAPTER TWELVE

AFTER THE FIRE, MY dad was going to look up Fitzpatrick. I assured him that I was fine, just a little shaken up. I put Zach to bed and started stirring up cookie dough.

The next day, although bleary-eyed and grumpy, I helped Zach get ready for school. Zach gave me a hug that lasted just a little too long as he climbed out of the car. I think seeing his mom being dragged out of a fire the night before scared him. He had already lost one parent, and the prospect of losing another was just about as earth-shaking as it gets for a little guy. He had been so tired last night that he fell asleep in the car on the way home. This morning, his mood was quiet as he sat at the table eating his cereal. The silence between us made me aware that I needed to be careful not to scare him like that again.

I, too, had eaten breakfast with only one parent for many years. While my dad had always been there for me, my mother had not. She left one day and never returned. Needing personal space and a life with someone else, she left me behind. With one parent left and a heaping helping of abandonment issues, I became overly protective of my dad. Every time he would go to work, I was worried he would get shot. I even asked him to switch jobs to something bullet-free, like a salesman or a barber. He knew I was scared and would comfort me with the low crime statistics of Pecan Bayou. He told me that he was still waiting to use his first bullet.

Without a mother I felt like I had a big hole in my life, and that was where my Aunt Maggie stepped in. She had been thirteen years old when my father was born, so he kind of treated her like his aunt, as well. Aunt Maggie was there to make my Halloween costumes and prom dresses. She was also there to help me through all the clumsy years of growing into a woman.

After Danny was born, my aunt and uncle were advised by the doctors not to have any more children. Now we know the chances of having two children with Down syndrome are almost nonexistent, but she and Uncle Jeeter heeded the warning. So Aunt Maggie and I found each other. I had a mother I wasn't supposed to have, and she had the little girl she hadn't been allowed to have. My father almost never complained about her presence, except for the time she forbade me to ride in the patrol car when he arrested people. Growing up a cop's daughter introduced me to a world other children only saw on television. I knew I was a little different when I announced to my third-grade teacher that I was putting an APB out when the class hamster went missing.

Now I was presented with another mystery. This time I might be able to find out where Barry was, and on top of that, I might be able to help Maggie. Breaking into Canfield's office gleaned more information than I had dreamed of. I tried remembering the names on the credit cards. Maybe I could try to contact some of these ladies and find out why they had given their credit cards to him. It was especially intriguing that all the cards belonged to women. Some men might have only women for friends, but Canfield didn't strike me as the type. I didn't even find him physically attractive. In his forties, he did have a decent head of black hair, but he had a round face with a barrel chest and always seemed to be mopping his brow with a handkerchief. Not exactly a chick magnet.

If I could ever get Maureen Boyle to quit condemning me and my family, I was sure she could provide some answers. She had to have been out at that hospital because of some connection to Canfield.

I decided to deliver my four dozen cookies personally to Benny at the barbecue. I pulled up, noticing a couple of foolhardy tourists sitting and sweating in the rocking chairs. Perhaps they were enjoying the Texas heat before returning to colder climates. Benny was stacking plates in a dishpan when I entered, juggling my cookies in plastic containers.

"Let me get those for you," he said as he put a plate in the stack and then came over to grab a couple of containers.

"My son informed me that he bragged about my cookie baking at the meeting and that I was to deliver them today."

Benny laughed. "Yes, I do recall hearing something about your ability in the kitchen. We are so grateful to have them, Betsy." He opened up a plastic lid and sampled one. "Say, these are good. If you ever decide to give up writing and want a job in my kitchen, I think we could work something out." He smiled as he chewed a peppermint chocolate chip cookie.

"I'm glad you stopped by." He put his hand on my shoulder. "I'm really sorry about what that boy said to Zach at the meeting. How is he doing?"

"He's all right, I guess. You know, he still thinks Barry will come back."

"Ah, yes. Hope springs eternal when you're that age. It's hard to learn that sometimes things just aren't going to go your way, no matter how angry or disgusted you may get." I wondered if we were still talking about Zachary. He continued. "I suppose you heard that I would like to put Zach together with the new boy, Tyler, as a camping buddy."

"I heard. Are you sure that's such a good idea?"

"I know, I know, but sometimes the best way to get two kids to get along is to make them work as a team. They'll have to sort out their differences just trying to get that tent up together."

I thought it was a terrific experience for the other kid but not so much for mine. Benny crossed his arms over his white barbecue apron and waited.

I relented. "If you think it will work, I guess so. But do me a favor and keep an eye on them, okay?"

"Sure," he said. I trusted him and knew he would take care of Zach. Hopefully he trusted me.

"Hey, I was just kind of wondering about something."

"Shoot."

Funny he should use that word, I thought. "I saw the contract you had with Oliver Canfield. That was what you were talking about when I asked you about the picture over there." I looked again to the picture, this time recognizing Oliver Canfield as he held a giant pair of scissors to cut the red ribbon stretched across the door.

Benny's face straightened. He scratched his ear. "He came up with this idea to refinance the restaurant after the last hurricane blew through. The winds took off the front facade of the building, and we were afraid we were going to have to close down. Seems like back then they were handing out mortgage deals like free toasters at the bank. When the rate adjusted to a higher payment, it was much more than we had in the monthly budget. That was why I asked you to help think of ways to cut costs and save money. I'm running awful close every month, and now with the new baby, Canfield shows up again. This time he tells me that, for a percentage of the business, he would be glad to help out a friend. A friend, he says. He wasn't any friend of mine."

He picked up a plate and started cleaning tables again. "Mr. Canfield was a sly one. I can't say that I am too upset about his passing."

"Meaning?"

"Meaning I worked my tail off here trying to make this a good restaurant and a way to support my family. I get up early and work until late. I can see the fruits of my labor every day. Canfield saw the fruits of my labor, too, and did all he could do to take them off of me."

"I'm beginning to think Canfield had a scam going with lots of people, Benny. You were just the one whose contract was found on his body."

Benny sat down in a booth, suddenly looking very tired. "I didn't know what to do. I put him off for a while, but he just kept calling. When Benny Jr. broke his foot and it looked as if they were going to have to do surgery, I just knew I had to do something. Affording health insurance when you're self-employed is next to impossible. He brought out a contract, and I signed it."

Benny got quiet as he contemplated his deal with the devil. Canfield had been Benny's own personal hurricane. He swooped in, damaged everything in sight and left Benny to clean up the mess. Benny sighed and looked up at me. I wondered if he was desperate enough to kill because of what had happened to him.

The bell on the restaurant door jingled behind us.

"Dr. Mac!" Benny said, rising and walking towards the counter. "I have your order of brisket ready for the Halloween party at the hospital."

This was just the person I had wanted to see. I had hopes of convincing him to let us resume the paranormal investigation. He thought I was there picking up an order of my own and stepped back.

"I'll wait until you help Betsy here."

"No," I said. "I wasn't in line. Dr. Mac, I'm really glad I ran into you."

He scratched his chin and furrowed his brow. "Trouble with Zach's arm?"

"No, he's fine. Thank you for asking."

A look of recognition came into his eyes. "Would this have something to do with all the hubbub at the town council meeting?"

"Yes," I admitted. "We are hoping you will agree to let us do the investigation out at the old hospital."

"So sad about the man who died out there."

"The man who died out there was a crook, Dr. Mac. Did you know that about him?" Benny asked.

Dr. MacPhee was surprised by Benny's statement. "Really? I hadn't heard anything about the man's character."

"He was fixin' to take a pretty good chunk of my profit every month. Now I'm thinking it might have been cheaper to file for bankruptcy."

"But I have to ask you Benny, now that you don't have Canfield making up the part of the payment you couldn't pay, how are you going to pay it?" I asked.

"I'm going to keep cooking and selling the best barbecue in Pecan Bayou. Isn't that right, Doc?"

"And if that isn't enough?" I asked.

He smiled and shrugged his shoulders. "I guess that's where faith comes in. Even though I may be listing out to sea, it's still better than being circled by a shark."

I had to agree. Dr. Mac peeled off some bills for Benny and started toward the door.

"Um, Dr. Mac, could I speak with you for just one moment?"

"Well, certainly my dear, if you don't mind walking me out to my car. I have a lot of hungry people to feed," he joked.

His voice was gentle, the same voice I remembered so many years ago, getting me through the toughest time in my life. He had been so supportive in the operating room. He made me feel as if I didn't need Barry to be my labor coach at all. It was just him and me – the screaming one who kept asking for more drugs.

"I know I'm repeating myself. But by letting us do this investigation, it would mean so much to my aunt."

"Oh?" he asked.

"Yes, you saw how upset she was getting at the meeting? Those things Miss Boyle said were not in any way true."

"I had a feeling about that," he said as he tucked the boxes of barbecue securely in the back seat of his Lincoln Town Car.

I wasn't sure of what Dr. Mac would think of Aunt Maggie's attitude toward the paranormal. "You see, my uncle died a few years back, and she just feels ..."

"That if she can find some spirits in the old hospital, that her own husband might be ... reachable?"

He patted my arm gently. "This is common, my dear. In my profession, I often deal with people feeling a great loss for their loved ones. They will do anything to get them back, it seems. If truth be told, I would do anything short of voodoo to get them back for them, but sometimes it's just not possible."

"Well, then maybe you do understand why we really want this investigation to proceed."

"I do," he said.

"That's great." I felt relief surging through me. He didn't think my aunt and her friends were all a bunch of crackpots.

"But I also feel it's my responsibility to listen to what Miss Boyle has to say about the negative influence airing this program may promote."

And like any reasonable judge, he was willing to hear both sides. Darn it.

I continued. "This program is harmless. Honestly, I can't say that I'm totally sold on the whole ghost hunting thing, but Aunt Maggie is."

His blue eyes twinkled. "You see, my dear, being on the town council is quite a job. Above everything, I have to be fair and make the right decision. I'm really glad you spoke to me about this today. This gives me some more insight into the situation. The best I can tell you is, now fully informed, I will give this some thought before the meeting this afternoon."

"Thanks, Dr. Mac." I knew he would think out the situation squarely and make the right decision.

CHAPTER THIRTEEN

WHEN I WALKED INTO the town council chambers a couple of hours later, Leo Fitzpatrick was waiting in the front row.

"Mr. Fitzpatrick," I said, nodding.

"Mrs. Livingston, I presume," he said, using a joke I had heard too many times. "Discover any bodies lately?"

"Rescue anyone from a burning building?" I countered.

"No, but I haven't been snooping in anybody's office either. Just exactly what where you doing in there?"

"I was about to ask you the same thing."

"Well, I'll tell you my story when you tell me yours," he answered. It wasn't the answer I was looking for, but it seemed it was all I was going to get out of him. Today he was here alone as both of our sons were sitting in class over at Buzz Aldrin Elementary. Hopefully nobody had to pull them apart today.

"Perhaps we can discuss it tonight at dinner."

"I can't wait," he said. Somehow his enthusiasm didn't seem genuine.

"My thoughts exactly. I don't really know why you were there at the bank building the same time I was, but, well … thank you for all that you did."

"No problem. I was going to get a complex if a second person I found in an empty building came up dead."

"Thanks to you, I didn't. By the way, would you have any idea why Canfield might have a drawer full of other people's credit cards?"

Fitzpatrick's gaze hardened.

"I can only imagine," he responded. Aunt Maggie walked in and grabbed me by the arm, pulling me away from Mr. Fitzpatrick.

"Guess what?" Aunt Maggie whispered.

"What?"

"Stanley has increased the power of the TV transmitter so now we will be shown all over Texas. Isn't that exciting?"

"You betcha." I wasn't feeling it.

As we walked away, Maggie pulled my arm again and whispered in my ear, "I think that man likes you."

"Great," I answered in disgust.

"What's wrong with him? I think he's kind of cute. He reminds me of my Jeeter when he was young."

"Wait until you meet his son."

The members of the town council entered and took their seats on the dais. Miss Boyle, who had been sitting straight-backed in the front row, smoothed out her crisp black pantsuit and looked down at her plain but finely manicured nails. She glanced around the room until she saw us sitting a few rows back. Her face took on a pucker, not unlike someone tasting a lemon. Tom Schuller called the meeting to order.

"I am calling this emergency meeting of the Pecan Bayou Town Council to order," he said, pounding the table with a wooden gavel. "Miss Boyle, we are about to give our decision on permitting access to the paranormal group out at the Johnson Tuberculosis Hospital. Is there anything you would like to add?"

"Yes, Mr. Schuller. As you know ..." But before she could continue, Howard came barreling into the room with a stack of discombobulated papers squeezed in between various volumes of paranormal science. Howard seemed to have found his courage today, and he meant to fight our case with lots and lots of reference materials. He had dressed for the occasion with a tan corduroy jacket complete with elbow patches and a pair of weathered blue jeans. He had to be burning up in that outfit, but at least today he sort of looked like a professor. Beads of sweat shone above his top lip.

"Sorry, folks," Howard said, bowing repeatedly as he backed into a folding chair.

Miss Boyle cleared her throat as if to quiet Howard in both sound and motion. "As I was saying – we are all aware of a bogus paranormal seance set to be filmed in the next twenty-four hours and then shown to the good people of this town through NUTV."

"Miss Boyle," Howard interrupted, "I'm afraid I must disagree with you on several points. First of all our investigation is not bogus, as you call it, and we're not holding a ..."

Miss Boyle interrupted back, "Whatever you choose to call your escapades is up to you, Mr. Gunther." Miss Boyle raised her hand to shoo him away like a pesky housefly. She looked over at Dr. Mac on the dais, who looked a bit overwhelmed by the speed of the responses coming from the two of them. Miss Boyle seemed to be looking to the council to shut Howard up.

"Oh...yes," Dr. Mac said as he picked up his cue, a little late. "Please, continue Ms. Boyle. Mr. Gunther, we will give you the opportunity to comment at the end of her statement."

"Thank you," she nodded toward the council members, her angular nose bobbing up and down. "Upon checking the archives of the Pecan Bayou paper, the police blotter reveals many incidents out at this hospital involving the youth of our town. I have requested your decision to stop the filming as it will only serve to excite our teenagers and cause God knows what else out there."

Before she had attacked the investigation on the merits of Satan worship, but now she was talking about a negative influence on the kids? I didn't know what Maureen Boyle's motivation was, but it seemed to be driving her to come up with better and better ideas to stop Aunt Maggie's group.

Maggie rustled beside me. "Your honor? May I say something?"

Don Schuller looked over at Maggie as he played with his ink pen. "Um, yes, you can come down here to the podium, Maggie."

Maggie rose and walked down to the wooden podium to face the Schuller brothers and Dr. MacPhee. Howard got up and readjusted the microphone for her again. "I have belonged to the Pecan Bayou Paranormal Society for five years now. We have spent many hours preparing for this investigation, and I would like to assure you that everything we do is strictly on a professional basis. We are hoping that, through our efforts, the people of this town will acknowledge the history of the hospital, as well as respect the ones who worked and died out there. Hopefully this will end the shenanigans, not make them worse."

Howard continued, "And if I may add something here, it seems that, at every turn of this process, we seem to be blocked by Miss Boyle."

Miss Boyle's face turned fiercely towards us. "And if I may say something, not only is your investigation frivolous, satanic and dangerous, there has already been a murder associated with it." She smirked. "What do you say to that, Mr. Gunther?"

Fitzpatrick stood up from his folding chair, "Excuse me, but I think you are looking at the hospital site incorrectly. What Miss Boyle says does have some merit to it. If someone wasn't experienced walking around an old building like that, he or she could come to some serious harm."

Miss Boyle raised her eyebrows and looked toward Howard and Maggie. Her triumphant look was not missed by Fitzpatrick.

He continued. "That being said, I think the town should not only back the investigation, but use it to further interests of investors to the property. It would be an ideal spot for a medical complex, a mall, or even some sort of entertainment venue like an amusement park. All you would need to do is to put a little commercial for the property at the end of the program."

Miss Boyle's mouth hung open.

The Schuller brothers' ears seemed to perk up at the idea of using the program to support a profit-making venture. The two of them nodded to each other and then began whispering.

"Am I to understand," demanded Miss Boyle, regaining her composure, "that you would advertise a building that will ultimately attract the wrong sort of people to a crime scene? Is there no respect for the dead in this town? You would use a scene of so much death to put on a tawdry commercial to promote some half-baked get-rich-quick scheme? Mr. Canfield, for all of his faults, was a person, after all."

"That is true," said Dr. Mac. I could tell he genuinely felt sorry for Miss Boyle and the dead Mr. Canfield. Mac always had a loving heart and tended to help out the underdog. Did he consider Miss Boyle the underdog?

"And so the whole idea of a paranormal program would do nothing to preserve Mr. Canfield's – dignity. When you put it that way, the idea of a commercial advertisement is simply repulsive." Dr. Mac said.

I raised my hand. "Excuse me, but the discovery of Mr. Canfield's body had nothing to do with the visit by the paranormal society."

"That is correct." Chief of Police Arvin Wilson had slipped in sometime while I was focused on Maggie. "Mr. Canfield's murder has nothing to do with my brother-in-law Howard and his group." Maggie and I both turned to look at Howard. Funny how he had never mentioned he was related to the chief of police. Arvin Wilson's lips turned up slightly and he smiled in Howard's direction. I'll bet he didn't know when he courted his lovely Alma thirty years ago there was such a wacko in the gene pool as her brother Howard.

"But," said Miss Boyle, "you do acknowledge the fact that this is a crime scene."

Wilson fingered the rim of his Stetson. "Yes, part of the hospital is a crime scene, but the paranormal team has promised to utilize other parts of the hospital for their investigation."

Miss Boyle continued. "What we need of the esteemed members of the council is a vote on whether or not this travesty of common decency should be allowed out on those hallowed grounds."

Dr. Mac nodded. "Yes, I see," he said. "Well, I believe we are ready for a vote." He looked over at me and Aunt Maggie and gave a slight smile. I felt reassured and thought of how he had expressed wanting to help people who were missing their loved ones. If the Schuller brothers agreed, it was a done deal.

"Yes, Dr. MacPhee, Tom and I both agree," said Don Schuller. He was wearing a rather large version of a Pecan Bayou High School football jersey. His son was a quarterback on the football team, and no doubt his concerns were straying towards tonight's game.

"Yes," his brother Tom said, "Don and I have discussed it, and," he smiled at Maggie, "we think the idea of a program out there is harmless, and we're looking forward to it. I've always wondered if that place was really haunted. We're fixin' to give you a chance to prove it ..."

Maggie and I jumped as Tom Schuller continued. "... as long as it ends with a nice commercial to promote the sale of the property." The crowd mumbled. Miss Boyle crossed her arms defiantly and turned her gaze on Maggie and Howard.

The other Schuller spoke next. "Tom and I both believe it will be a source of positive revenue for the town, eventually." Howard jumped, accidentally knocking his papers and books to the floor. Tom Schuller pounded the gavel.

"And I will also vote in the affirmative," Dr. Mac added, as if it mattered.

Miss Boyle stood up quietly and walked over to Maggie and me as we rose to leave. "This is not over," she said.

"I think the council just agreed it is," I returned.

"There are things you do that will be judged by a different court."

"Yeah, well it's a little too late to get on Judge Judy," Maggie said.

CHAPTER FOURTEEN

A FEW HOURS LATER, the scent of garlic, onions, tomatoes and peppers wafted throughout the house as I stirred spaghetti sauce. Zach hadn't spoken much since he got home from school. Minutes after coming through the door, he plopped down on the couch and took solace by leading two little Italian men named Mario and Luigi through impossible video game feats. I had the feeling all of this was getting to be a little much for him.

He hadn't responded well when I told him that I had invited Leo Fitzpatrick and his son Tyler to dinner.

"You invited them? Why would you do that?"

"Tyler is going to be your buddy at the campout, and I just wanted to make sure you guys are getting along."

"You have to call Mr. Benny. I can't be a buddy to Tyler." His little voice shrieked upwards. "He'll kill me!"

"No, he won't. I had lunch with his dad the other day, and Tyler's been going through some rough times."

"You had lunch with Mr. Fitzpatrick? Tyler's dad? Like a date?"

"No. Not like a date. We just both happened to be at Birdies Diner at lunch time and decided to sit together."

He didn't look appeased by that. He tilted his head slightly evaluating me for truthfulness. "By the window?"

"Yes."

"Where everyone could see?"

"Yes, already, but it wasn't a date. I promise." I crossed my heart with two fingers.

"I don't want Dad to come back and see you sitting at the diner with some other dad. He could turn around and go away again."

I drew in a breath and felt a pit in my stomach. Just when I had let myself forget about it, Barry's rejection was there. Here was his son, petrified that if we didn't do anything but wait, he would punish us by leaving again. That is, if he ever showed up. I suppose Zach got that attitude from me. He had seen me waiting for Barry for seven years. The only time I went "out" was with my family. There were no men threatening to take his place – until this week. Somehow, I broke an unspoken code between the two of us. I ventured out into the world. Zach still had his candle in the window burning for his dad. I had just doused mine with a bucket of cold water.

I remembered how Tyler had mocked him heartlessly about his dad and wondered how many other comments had been hurled at him in the viciousness of childhood teasing. If it had been happening, he didn't complain about it. I knew no matter what other kids said to him, or even what I said to him, he would never give up on his dad. I could see it in his eyes, every holiday and every birthday. He would spend a little time by the window, expecting to see his father walking down the driveway, gravel crunching at his feet, a plastic bag filled with cough drops swinging from his hand. I was pretty sure he thought it was his own little secret. Yet he would give little clues about what was on his mind by finding those times to ask questions about his missing father. What color was Dad's hair? Did he like sports? Could he throw a football? All of those things would come sneaking out when he was trying to keep his inner thoughts quiet. So I would smile and sit him down away from the window and tell him a little about his dad. I could tell him if his dad liked sports and could throw a football, but the one thing I seemed to never tell him was why Barry didn't come back.

I probably did him a disservice by not telling him the awful things about Barry. What do you say to a child? "Oh, your dad was a great football player, and by the way, he skipped town, left a pregnant wife, and put our little family in some pretty serious debt. What a guy!"

I couldn't even tell him whether the reason that Barry didn't return had to do with us or with some sort of foul play that nobody had figured out yet. I wanted to hug the hurt away, but knew I didn't have the cure that would heal this. Having other male role models in his life helped some, but they were just a stand-in for what he actually needed. Learning to make a friend out of a bully seemed to me to be one of those jobs in the dad column, but once again, it fell into mine. As the time neared for our dinner guests to arrive, I called to Zach, who was still in front of the TV.

"Zach, come set the table for dinner. Tyler and his father will be here soon."

He groaned. "Okay Mom, just give me one more minute."

"All right, but not too long." I knew by now that giving Zach one more minute was infinitely better than an all-out war over video games. No matter what was going on, he would need another minute and would come around the corner in the allotted time. I could be saying, "Zach, the house is on fire, and he would return with something like, 'Sure thing, Mom, just one more minute. Let me get to the portal.'"

A minute later Zach walked in, rolled his eyes, let out a sigh and stuck his hands out. I handed him a stack of plates with silverware and napkins stacked on top. He began to set the places at the table slowly, his mind on something else.

"Hey, Mom," he said as he placed the silverware crookedly on a napkin. "I was just wondering. Does Grandpa still look for Dad?"

A leaf of lettuce escaped from the bowl as I tossed the salad. "You bet, champ."

"Good," he said, a quietness creeping into his voice.

"You going to be okay with Tyler coming over here tonight?"

"No."

"Come on, we have to try."

"You don't understand, Mom. Tyler is a mean boy. He's been mean since the day he started at school."

"Well, maybe he just needs a friend."

"A friend to beat up all the time?"

"No," I corrected him. "A friend to find out why he's so angry all the time. Maybe he misses his mom."

That made him think a minute, but then a scowl came over his face as the doorbell chimed. As Fitzpatrick came in the door, he handed me a bottle of Riesling. "This is for our supper tonight. Thank you so much for inviting us."

"We're just glad you could come," I said. The boys eyed each other, reminding me of the predatory animals on the nature channel.

Shortly after sitting around the table, all three of my fellow diners dug into the spaghetti dinner. I surmised that Tyler and his dad didn't get a whole lot of home cooking, or else they were just downright hungry. They scarfed it down.

"So are you looking forward to the campout tomorrow night, Tyler?" I asked when it seemed he had come up for air.

Tyler was scooping more pasta into his mouth. "Sure," he said through a mouthful.

"So with your ... situation ... Benny watches out for Zach?" Fitzpatrick asked.

"Sometimes. My dad goes with Zach when he's not on duty."

"And he'll be on duty on Halloween?"

"Oh, yes," I replied. "Will he ever. Between the Scouts in the woods, the protection of the crime scene, the paranormal investigation and then all of the other pranks that go on at Halloween, he's pretty over-scheduled."

"I bet. Did they ever find out who murdered that guy, Canfield?"

"No, not yet."

"It's all pretty strange how I ran into him." Fitzpatrick twirled his spaghetti. I expected him to continue, but he did not.

"You saw Mr. Canfield before he died?" Zach asked.

Fitzpatrick looked at me, checking to see if he could reveal his part in the day of Canfield's death. Unseen to Zach, I quietly nodded in agreement.

"Oh, that." He sat back for a minute and looked up. "Well, I was out walking around the hospital, scouting it out for my investment client from Dallas, when I turned a corner and there he was. He about jumped out of his skin when he saw me. A guy like Canfield probably needed to watch his own back for all the people he's swindled out there."

"Wow," Zach said, with Tyler echoing him.

"I've heard some things about that but really no details. Do you know of any incidents where he took someone's money?" I asked.

"Um ... I don't know. I just wouldn't trust him," he said.

"Well, thank goodness you gave the council an idea on how to sell that old eyesore. You saved the day and my aunt's investigation show. I thought it would be canceled, especially with all that stuff Miss Boyle was saying."

"It's amazing to me how heated up she gets about all of that hocus pocus."

"Yes, I know."

I noticed Zach and Tyler had both finished their meals. "Mom, can Tyler and I go play video games?"

"It's all right with me, how about you?" I gestured to Fitzpatrick.

"Leo, please?" said Tyler. "Uh, I mean, please Dad?"

"Sure."

Tyler jumped up, knocking Zach sideways and hitting him in the cast.

"Sorry," Tyler said. The two boys rushed off to the next room.

Fitzpatrick folded his napkin in his lap. His eyes darted to me. "Tyler's still getting used to calling me Dad. His mother always called me Leo in front of him. I'm hoping the campout this weekend will help things along a bit."

I nodded. "Yes, I wonder how Zach would react if Barry came back into our lives. He probably wouldn't know what to call him, either."

"I promised Benny I would serve as sort of a second in command. It doesn't help that the Texas Piney Woods seem to have brought out the hay fever in me. I'll probably be sneezing and coughing all night. It must have affected Canfield too – I heard him coughing all throughout that old place."

"I just can't believe you were out at the old hospital on the day that Canfield was killed. You're probably the last person to see him alive."

"Correction. I'm probably the last person to see Canfield before his killer."

"Yes, you're right." I laughed uneasily.

"Besides, I saw Benny Mason pull up and walk off into the woods."

"You did?"

"Yes, but I never saw him inside where we were."

"Did you tell my father this?"

"No. I didn't know I needed to. We did have quite a conversation ending with the ever-popular 'Don't leave town.'"

"You need to tell him this, right away, for Benny's sake."

I recited my dad's phone number to Fitzpatrick. Upon calling him, he proceeded to repeat to him what he had just shared with me. I wasn't sure whether this would clear Benny or just get a witness confirming he was out there.

"Yes. Well, thank you, Lieutenant Kelsey." He pushed the end button on his cell phone. I had started rinsing plates and putting them in the dishwasher. Fitzpatrick refilled our wine glasses and brought mine over to me.

"What did he say?" I asked.

"He said thank you for the information but that he already knew Benny was out there. Benny told him that he was out there."

"He did, but my dad didn't have anyone else saying he was out there," I said, sipping my wine.

"Benny is a nice guy and all, but what if he really did it?"

I thought about that for a moment. Things like that do happen. Sometimes the charming guy who works with kids ends up being some kind of psychopath who kills the butcher because he didn't cut enough fat off the brisket. No, not Benny. I had seen him so many times in stressful situations with the Scouts, and nothing seemed to crack his patience. He just wasn't the killer type.

"But what if he didn't?" I asked. "What's going to happen to Celia and the boys if he goes off to prison for a crime he didn't commit? What's going to happen to their business?"

"I guess you're right. Would it help to tell you that I saw him drive away while Canfield was still alive?"

I went over to the table where he had laid down his cell phone, picked it up and handed it to him. "Call him back."

He was stunned. "Uh, okay." After speaking with my dad on the phone for a few minutes, Fitzpatrick handed the phone to me.

"He said he wants to talk to you now."

"Hey, Dad. Isn't that great news about Benny?"

"Yes, darlin' it's great. Hey listen, I have a little question for you. Why are you entertaining one of my main suspects in the death of Oliver Canfield?"

I sat down on a high stool in my kitchen aware that Fitzpatrick was listening. "Um, Dad, we're having a play date."

"A what?"

"A play date, Dad."

"Well, after seven years I guess I should be pleased with whatever you're calling it," he said.

"No! Not like that. The boys will be camping buddies, so we're trying to get them to become better acquainted."

"Oh, so they don't kill each other."

"Something like that."

"Well, as long as you are looking out for your son with the boy, I need you to look out for yourself and that guy you're playdatin' with. I never did get too straight a scoop on just what he was doin' at that fire. As a matter of fact, I'm not all that sure I know what you were doin' out at the bank building."

"Dad. You were going to shut us out of the hospital, and well ... Don't laugh, okay? I wanted to see if I could figure out what Oliver Canfield was doing and to make sure that whatever had happened it didn't have anything to do with Barry."

"Barry? Too much time has passed for that, Betsy."

"Maybe. I know, Dad, I know. It sounds preposterous."

"And what did this private investigation prove? You have interfered with an ongoing investigation and put yourself in danger."

"Yes, but I may have figured why someone killed him."

"Do tell."

"Did you read through the stuff on his desk? The man had at least three different girlfriends."

"It might make him tired, but I don't think that's against the law."

"It is if Canfield was using their credit cards without their permission."

"Where did you find these credit cards? Why didn't you tell me about this sooner?" My father's anger was rising.

"I didn't know how you would react to my 'interfering,' dad. I found the cards hidden in his desk drawer."

"Did you happen to bring these cards out of the fire with you?"

"Well, no."

"Do you remember the names on the cards?"

"Um, let me think. Ruby Morris. Uh, Mary – no, Martha Johnson, and uh ... Baumgartner. The only one I knew was Maureen Boyle."

"*The* Maureen Boyle?"

"The one and only."

"OK, I'll check this out. In the meantime, you keep an eye on Fitzpatrick and son over there, and if there's any trouble they'll have to answer to your old dad."

Fitzpatrick leaned against the kitchen counter with his arms crossed, holding the half-empty wine glass. He watched me for a moment and then spoke as soon as I finished my conversation with my dad.

"Excuse me for listening in, but did you say you found something with the name Baumgartner on it in Canfield's office?"

I handed him back his phone. "Uh, yes. I don't know if my dad would want you to know, but then again, after hearing me talk about it, I guess you already know, now don't you?" I surmised.

Fitzpatrick looked a little confused after all that. He cocked his head to the side. "What do I know, exactly?"

I rubbed my eyes and felt a little tired, especially after that second glass of wine. "It was a credit card I found along with a few others with all with the names of women on them. Do you know someone named Baumgartner? And as long as I'm thinking about it, just what were you doing there besides rescuing me?"

"I was wondering when we would get around to that, you see ..."

A screech came from the living room. "Mom! Tyler won't share!"

We put down our wine glasses and headed for the living room.

"Tyler, it's my turn."

Tyler was bent over the game controller pushing buttons as his body swerved with a race car careening down drawn-in highways on the television screen.

"In a minute, dude."

"Tyler!" Fitzpatrick said, his tone commanding. "Put down the controller this minute and apologize to our host."

Tyler's car crashed into a wall on the screen, generating the "Game Over" banner.

Tyler stuffed the controller back into Zach's hands. "Sorry." His apology was short and unfeeling. He rose to Fitzpatrick's side. "Can we go now?"

"Sure," Fitzpatrick answered as he followed Tyler to the door.

"But you were about to tell me why you were in the bank building," I said after him.

"Oh yeah, well, I guess I was just there to rescue you." He put his fingers to his forehead as if touching an invisible brim of a hat. "Thank you for a lovely dinner, Mrs. Livingston. We'll see the both of you at the campout."

"

CHAPTER FIFTEEN

THE NEXT DAY, I DROPPED Zach for the campout. He was dressed in his policeman's uniform — heavily altered with safety pins — which consisted of his Scout shorts, along with one of my dad's old shirts tucked in so far the hem that it could be seen creeping out where the shorts hit his legs. That shirt was important, Zach told me, because it had PBPD patches on the sleeve. It was official, whereas all the other kids had on fake stuff. He would be there as a Scout but also operating as a junior deputy for the campout. Barney Fife lives and breathes right here in Texas, complete with one spitwad in his pocket.

The sun was beating down as we unloaded his gear at the campsite. I could smell bug repellent drifting by as all the little boys ran around us, laden with bundled sleeping bags and tents. Rivers of sweat ran down through their hair, causing it to layer in straight lines across their foreheads.

I was not excited about leaving Zach with his camping buddy the bully, but what could I do? Maybe Tyler would think Zach could actually arrest him if he beat him up. Hopefully Benny would keep an eye on them, or at least listen for screams. Zach assured me that he could take care of himself and didn't need Benny babysitting him. Fifty pounds of fighting man, or at least that's what he thought of himself.

When I met up with Maggie and Danny in front of the hospital, I couldn't help but notice Maggie's hair. As she walked over to me, her bouffant style seemed to be molded around her "Paranormal Investigator" cap. She even had a "Casper the Friendly Ghost" pin stuck on the brim of the hat, just in case it might attract a few spirits. It was a work of hair art. I raised my eyebrows and crooked my neck around trying to see the whole thing.

"Aunt Maggie? Did you have your hair done?"

"Do you like it? I had Ruby Green down at The Best Little Hair House fix it up for me. No matter what happens tonight, every hair will stay in place."

"Miss Ruby used a whole can of hairspray," Danny added.

I would have to remember the "no open flames" policy around Aunt Maggie tonight.

"But that's not the best part," Maggie continued. "While I was gettin' my hair done, some of the ladies were asking me about finding Mr. Canfield. Seems they all wanted to know about it."

I didn't think Danny knew all the details of his mother and me finding a body. That kind of thing might upset him, especially after he had been the one to find my uncle, his father, dead. He had nightmares about it for months afterward. "Well, once we started talking about that, the ladies started sharing their own haunted experiences. It seems just about everyone in this town has a ghost story of some sort. The dead are haunting all of us, my dear."

I thought of Barry. The living weren't doing too bad a job, either.

"So by the time Ruby got my hair piled up and sprayed around this hat, I had three more volunteers to help us out on Halloween."

"You did?"

"I sure did. The Pecan Bayou Paranormal Society's newest members are Anna Harrel, that clerk from the grocery, Ruby, and Lily MacPhee, Dr. MacPhee's wife. She said she looked forward to having some fun this weekend after all they been doin' for their daughter's upcomin' wedding."

It would be great to have some extra people to carry gear, and if luck was on my side, one of those people would be assigned the dead tunnel. I would happily stay outside in NUTV's van drinking sweet tea out of a thermos all night. I was beginning to think my favorite way to view ghosts was on my television set at home. I could hide under a blanket when the violins started playing and the heroine suddenly found herself all alone. The real-life version of this somehow wasn't quite as much fun.

Half an hour later, after the NUTV van arrived, we were trudging across the grounds under the baking sun. "Hurry up, Betsy. We have to get all these lights set up before dusk," said Aunt Maggie.

I hustled along behind my aunt, who was now dressed in the full regalia of a ghost hunter. She had a fifty-foot extension cord slung over the shoulder of her black knit top. She also had on her ghost buster belt, complete with an EVP device strapped on, as well as her flip camera and flashlight. She had insisted that I also wear my hat, so I put my hair into a ponytail to eliminate that "all your hair crammed into a hat" look. I chose to wear my yearly favorite, a black glow-in-the-dark jack-o-lantern shirt, along with black jeans. I actually tossed around the idea of wearing shorts for the heat, but I knew walking through the endless spider webs in this place would have my skin crawling. I already regretted my decision as I felt the sweat on my skin. Hopefully when the sun went down we would at least get a breeze.

Howard stood in front of the aged structure with two portable lights shining on him as he described the history of the hospital. Today he actually looked sedate wearing a black t-shirt and black shorts. I thought maybe his fashion sense had bowed to necessity until I saw his black and orange argyle socks resting mid-calf on his legs. Stanley had brought over a crew of four to film the show. He crossed his arms and nodded his head as he watched the filming of Howard describing the hospital. I just hoped Howard wasn't doing that thing where his eyes bugged out like he did at the town council. If he did, no one would watch to the end of the show where the council hoped for its glorious commercial.

We had been told to steer clear of the second-floor room where Oliver Canfield had been murdered. We would stay on the main floor, mostly concentrating on the rooms situated there, including the cafeteria, two hallways of patient rooms and the morgue. We put the lights down and headed back to the van.

I could see many cars now parked along the road. It had to be a mixture of the Scout parents and the people attending the filming of the investigation. Less than a mile or so from this hospital was the new Pecan Bayou Hospital. Howard had mentioned that the sounds of the ambulance sirens could interfere with filming. At least if there was an accident at the campout, medical help would be close by.

I sat on the bumper of the van, waiting for my next set of directions from Maggie or Howard and slapping at a mosquito trying to suck blood out of my exposed arm. As the sun started its daily descent, the mosquito population put on their vampire fangs. I knew there was mosquito repellent in the front seat of the van and made my way around. I ran smack into Aunt Maggie, whose animated face told me something was up.

"I'm being asked to say a few words on camera," Maggie said, a slight excited quiver in her voice. "Can you take these things over to the main hallway?"

I picked up one more heavy bag and a suitcase of some sort while Maggie rushed off for her close-up. As I trudged from the van, wishing I had taken a moment to spray on some bug spray, I looked up at the towering windows of the old hospital. They seemed to be getting more elongated as the shadows stretched over their rectangular shapes. I looked to the window where I thought I had seen a ghost a few days ago. Could I have been looking at the murderer, or was it some sort of an apparition? Now that I was mere hours away from spending the night in a haunted hospital, my feelings on whether I believed in the whole other-world thing were coming to light. Did I believe there were beings walking around — or should I say floating around — in another dimension, or was it all just a bunch of hooey someone dreamed up while sitting around a campfire? As I came closer to the hospital, something flickered on the second floor. Something not that much different from what I had seen with Zach. I set down my load and yelled up into the hospital.

"Hello? Is someone up there?" I was immediately shushed by the film crew. Oops. I forgot my aunt was on camera. I had been directed by my dad not to go to the second level for any reason, but quite possibly someone else had not heeded the warning and was up there tromping through a crime scene. Where was George Beckman? Maybe he had taken a dinner break and somebody was up there sightseeing.

"Hello?" I repeated a little more softly this time. When no answer came back, I picked up my bags, set them inside the door and started ascending the stairway.

"George? Are you up here?" Again, no answer.

As I came into the large open solarium, the light from the late afternoon sun shone through the window frames, leaving a long shadow. The heat was stifling. I walked to the center of the solarium and stopped, not wanting to make a sound. I listened until I heard someone coughing and footsteps walking rapidly away from me, possibly down a hallway on the other side of the room. I crossed the solarium in pursuit as I heard the footsteps going down the darker passage. "You know you can't be up here! This area is off limits to anyone but the police ... Hello?"

Whoever it was, they didn't seem to care too much about my dire warning.

The footsteps picked up from a walk to a run, and I followed at a faster pace. We went on like this, rounding corners and running down the next hall. I felt the heat sapping my energy. The intruder stayed far ahead of me. I couldn't see who it was. I heard a doorway open at the end of the hall leading to the stairwell. The door slammed just as I got to it. Expecting to hear the sound of feet clumping down the stairs, I was surprised. It was now quiet.

Was the mystery intruder standing on the other side of the door? Were they getting ready to attack me? Maybe they thought they were in a suitable hiding place. I held my breath, and yanked open the rusty white door.

Nothing. Nobody was standing there waiting to attack. I couldn't see anybody on the stairwell, and there was no sound at all. Where did my intruder go? Had they crept out through the stairway fire exit door to the outside?

I ran down the stairs and burst through the outside door, hitting square on the chest of a person much taller than I was. I fell backwards and landed on my behind in the overgrown weeds outside the hospital. The intruder, whose face was blocked by the sun, was coming closer and closer towards me.

The intruder leaned down. I screamed and crawled backwards on my hands.

"Stop!" a male voice yelled. As the sun went behind a cloud, I looked up into the icy blue eyes of Leo Fitzpatrick.

"Mr. Fitzpatrick?"

"What is wrong with you?" he said, offering me his hand.

"What's wrong with you?" I repeated back to him. "What were you doing upstairs near the crime scene? Don't you know you're not supposed to be anywhere near it? What were you trying to do?"

"I wasn't trying to do anything."

"Why did you run from me then? I know it was you. I heard you coughing. You sounded like a two-pack a day smoker up there."

"I'm sorry, I don't know what you're talking about. I didn't run from you."

"Don't give me that. You ran through the second floor and then down the stairs."

"Betsy, you don't look good." His voice was gentle, and the blue eyes that looked so cold a minute ago softened. "When was the last time you had any water? It has to be over a hundred degrees on that second floor."

I felt my cheeks with my hands. "What?"

"You just came bounding out of that door as if you were being chased by a bear. You ran smack into me and then acted like I was going to attack you or something."

"You weren't?" I said, feeling dumb now.

"Sorry. Hate to disappoint you, but I was over here looking for firewood for the campsite." He seemed sincere, and yet there was something about this man I just didn't trust. Once again, he had shown up at just the right time.

"Looking for wood?"

He pulled a water bottle out of his pocket and handed it to me. "Here, this is a little warm now, but let's just sit down on the step and you can tell me all about it." I followed him back up the steps, plopped down and took a swig from his lukewarm water.

"That wasn't you?"

"No ma'am," he answered, shaking his head.

"If it wasn't you, then who was it?" I turned to face the door, now closed. "Did you see anybody else come out of this door?"

"No, again."

"If it wasn't you, then did who I chase through the hospital?" I took another drink as the sound of the cicadas rose in the woods.

"Well, when it comes to me, you can be assured you are safe." He said it, but I wasn't all that sure I believed him.

"Tell me about your investor for the hospital, Mr. Fitzpatrick. Tell me why you were at the fire," I said. Who was this man sitting here sharing his water with me? I had to know.

"What's to tell?" He gestured with both hands up. "It's just an investor."

"I don't think there's any kind of investor privacy law anywhere, so isn't there anything else you can tell me?"

He shifted slightly on the step. "I have to think of the privacy of this person. It's only common decency."

"Oh." He had an answer for everything, which always seemed to turn out to be nothing. I felt my frustration rising. I put the cap back on the water bottled and shoved it at him.

"And you just happened to, at this time of all times, be here at a torn-down hospital nobody's given a hoot about for decades on the same day that Oliver Canfield was here. Yeah, right."

Fitzpatrick looked down at this watch.

"I have to get back," he said, standing up.

"So you can gather wood to start a fire?" I asked, wondering if this would be the first or the second fire he was starting this week. After all someone had to start the fire at the bank, so why not him? What had he been trying to destroy in that office? Was he a part of whatever Canfield had been doing?

Fitzpatrick sniffed as the late afternoon breeze covered us in another layer of humidity.

"Lots to do." With that, he started walking back towards the woods. He turned around for one last word.

"You be careful in that old hospital. Bad things seem to happen to people in there."

CHAPTER SIXTEEN

I WALKED AROUND THE front of the building where the film crew continued working. I knew when I was getting the brush-off from Leo Fitzpatrick. Who was this investor? Why was he on Canfield's appointment calendar? There was no denying Fitzpatrick's charm, but he also had an element of danger to him. If I couldn't get him to crack, then maybe I could crack Tyler as well.

"So we will take two investigators and a camera and sound on each run tonight," Howard said. "We want to keep it as simple as possible and limit the possibility of human interference in our investigations."

I wondered if they would actually get anything on tape tonight. I had seen countless videos of floating forms playing on Aunt Maggie's computer and television. Would Howard and Stanley be able to get some kind of footage like that? We would have every kook in the country out here if that happened. Oliver Canfield's dream was coming true – we would be rich with investors. Too bad he wouldn't be here to see it all. Then again, maybe he was.

I headed to a cooler Stan had placed in the back of the van.

As Maggie and Danny were coming towards me, I picked up three water bottles from the icy confines of the cooler. "Water break, Aunt Maggie. Be right back."

"Okay, dear. You do look a little red in the face."

"Very important to drink water in the heat," said Danny.

I TRUDGED THROUGH THE woods over to the campsite to see Tyler. He and Zach were struggling to pound in tent stakes. They were surrounded by other little boys in various states of campsite readiness. The tents were set about ten feet apart between the trees towering above them.

"Pull it tight, shrimp," Tyler yelled to Zach from one side of the collapsed tent. Tyler had on a pirate costume, complete with eye patch and wobbling bird on his shoulder. His plastic sword hung from his belt as he tried to hammer a stake into the ground.

"Hey you guys, how about some water?"

"Thanks, Mom," Zach said, his little cheeks rosy pink and his hair plastered to his forehead.

"Thanks," said Tyler. We all sat down in front of the tent on a couple of logs the boys had laid out in a sort of bark-toned living room. "So Tyler, can I ask you a question?"

Tyler tipped the water bottle back to gulp, but his eyes turned to me. "Okay," he said, filtering out a burp in the process.

"How long have you been living with your dad?"

"My dad? ... Oh, my dad. I've just been with him for a little bit, since my mom ..."

I could tell he was getting uncomfortable talking about his home situation. I softened my approach. "Do you miss your mom?"

He looked down into the bottle as if the answer was waiting for him there. "Yes." His voice was barely audible.

There was quiet between us. This was a side of Tyler we hadn't seen, and it all came about when I mentioned his mom. Maybe the tough-guy thing was all about being homesick.

I was even more surprised when Zach, the victim of Tyler's taunts for the last week, chose to put his arm around him. "Gee, Tyler, you should have told me. Sometimes I miss my dad too. Even though I never really knew him and all," he added quickly.

"Yeah, well, I knew my mom," Tyler bit back.

Then, even more to my surprise, I saw a little tear bounce off his hand.

"I'm sorry. I didn't mean to upset you," I said.

"Leo says it's okay to cry about it sometimes, just not in front of other people. I feel stupid."

"It's not stupid. It's ... it's ... okay," Zachary said softly. I had so hoped the two boys would get along, but I never stopped to think about the fact that they shared a common loss of a parent.

"When was the last time you talked to her on the phone?" I asked. Tyler looked bewildered. Maybe he was so upset he didn't quite understand me.

"Tyler? Your dad does let you call her on the phone, right?" I began to wonder if this was an amicable arrangement or not. Maybe she wasn't answering his calls because she was so wound up in her new life. Some people just threw kids away, it seemed.

"Uh, you can't reach her by phone right now." That said it all. She was avoiding him. No wonder the kid was angry all the time. I made up my mind right then and there to be a new person to this boy.

"I see," I said. "I tell you what, Tyler. Anytime you feel like you need someone to talk to, you can call me, okay?"

"And me," said Zach, my partner in crime.

"Really?" Tyler looked up from the ground at me, his chubby hands holding the water bottle quietly in his lap.

"Really," I repeated.

"I have to ask Uncle Leo."

I thought about what Fitzpatrick had said about Tyler not being used to calling him dad. It was kind of sad because they were thrown together now. He had missed so many important things in Tyler's life. They hadn't had the time that Zach and I had to build our reliance and trust on one another. Once again, I had holes in Fitzpatrick's story, but at least I knew his kid wouldn't be beating up my kid all night long.

DURING THE REMAINDER of the afternoon, I kept thinking about Tyler's reaction to the mention of his mom. He had seemed like a tough kid at the Scout meeting, but one mention of his mother and he turned to jelly. So often the kid who is picking on yours has already been kicked around by someone bigger than himself.

"Okay, Betsy, in our segment we are going to be walking around the rooms in the 'C' corridor, down this hall," Aunt Maggie said. In the fading light of the afternoon, it just looked like another torn-down hallway, too sorry-looking to produce a sizable ghost. At the end of the hallway was the bottom of the stairway that I had just chased my invisible intruder down. Many of the doors were off the hinges, but a few still hung on by sheer rust alone. Above me, some of the cratered ceiling tiles of the '60s lay along their metal frameworks in a scattered fashion. Maggie continued to chatter about things she would be pointing out to me when we were on camera later. As I listened to her voice, I heard the undeniable sound of footsteps again, above our heads. This time, even though I expected it, there was no cough.

"Wait," I said, holding up my hand. "Do you hear that? That's what I heard earlier. Maybe whoever it was came back." We were on the south side of the hospital, and the crime scene, with its police officer standing guard, was on the north side. Why would someone be walking around up there? It was understandable that some Halloween prank might involve seeing a real crime scene, but what would entice someone to the other side of the building?

"What? I don't hear ..." she stopped mid-sentence as she, too, heard the footsteps above us.

"Who's upstairs? Boy howdy, Judd will have their hide."

I headed back to the door that led to the stairwell. Maybe if I could sneak up the stairs this time, I would catch whoever this was. I pulled open the security door, and a sizable rusty metal tube came hurtling down the stairs. Before I could get out of the way, it smacked right into me.

TWENTY MINUTES LATER I sat inside the back of an ambulance while the paramedics checked me out. "It's amazing you weren't hurt worse by that thing, Betsy," said Stanley. The television crew was trying hard to eliminate the sound of any ambulances and here they had to call one directly to the place they were filming.

Danny was standing by the door. "I'm surprised it didn't squash you like a bug."

I lifted my head to nod with a pained smile.

He continued, "I'm just glad my mom was there. It was your lucky day, Betsy."

"It certainly was." Maggie's eyes kept looking me over up and down as her hand patted my shoulder.

"Mom!" Zach ran across the field from out of the trees, followed by Tyler, Leo Fitzpatrick and Benny Mason. Benny stood with the rest of the Scouts, who were hovering on the edge of the woods.

"I'm okay," I told Zach as he barreled into me. We had to quit meeting like this.

"You don't look okay," said Fitzpatrick.

"Someone decided to try to get rid of us by throwing an old hot water heater on Betsy," said Maggie.

"Uncle Judd is looking around up there," Danny said to me. "If somebody's wandering around up there, he'll find them. He finds the bad guys." Danny and Zach nodded their heads in unison.

Maggie smiled. "He certainly will find whoever it is up there."

Stanley added, "It seems like at every turn something happens to stop the filming of this program."

Howard walked up now, running his hand through his flyaway gray hair.

Maggie held my hand. "We know a lot of people have been against this whole thing, but I didn't think anyone was mean enough to do this."

"So does this mean the investigation is off?" Howard asked.

"Howard ... Maggie ..." Stanley raised his eyebrows and let out a sigh. "I know you have your hearts set on this, but look at what we just went through. Are you sure this is a good idea? I might be able to work out some sort of a partial refund."

Howard tilted his head to the side, looking up at the old hospital. He turned to us with a rapid movement. "I know no one has thought of this, but this may be an action performed by a nonhuman."

Leo Fitzpatrick, who had been quiet, perked up at that one. "Nonhuman?" he said.

"Nonhuman?" Stanley echoed.

"Of course, this is the classic behavior of a poltergeist, or bad spirit. I think there might be a negative force that will do anything to keep us away."

"Well, what are we supposed to do about it?" I asked.

He shot a glance at Maggie, his eyes starting to bug out at the thought of it.

"Call a priest."

At that, my father walked out of the hospital with his hand tightly closed around the arm of none other than Miss Maureen Boyle.

"No need to call a priest. I think our attacker was quite alive."

CHAPTER SEVENTEEN

"MISS BOYLE?"

Today, the prim and proper Miss Boyle was out of her pencil skirt and had put on jeans and a gray t-shirt. She didn't seem to be too happy with her police escort.

"Seems like it," my father answered. "I found her trying to come down the stairs from the other side of the hospital."

"Is it against the law to come down the stairs now?" she asked.

Maggie was incensed. "It's one thing to insult me in front of the town, calling me a devil worshiper, but it is quite another when you throw a water heater at my niece." She rose from my side, and I was pretty sure she was about to swing a boilermaker at my attacker. I grabbed her hand to pull her back, although secretly I would have liked to see her do it.

"You people do not need to be here – and you have no proof I was the one who threw that rusty piece of metal down the stairs."

"Then let me ask you what you were doing upstairs in that heat?"

"It is absolutely none of your business what I was doing up there. You let your family run willy-nilly through the place. I don't see you arresting them," Miss Boyle said.

"Miss Boyle," Judd said. "Show us your hands."

Miss Boyle did not comply but simply stared at my father with a look of defiance. She was not budging as her eyes began to turn into slits staring at us through her glasses, now slightly askew. My father reached down and grabbed her hands and turned them palm up to all of us. From the dim light available, I could see something dark on both of them.

"Hmm, rust. Could it be from pushing a rusty piece of metal down the stairs?"

"I want to call my lawyer."

"And so you shall."

"I wish I had never met any of you people." Her lip was firm.

"I think you've made yourself quite clear on that point," I answered. "What is it that drives you so crazy about us being here? I just don't get it. Do you put razor blades in apples to discourage trick-or-treaters, too?"

"No!" she screamed. "No! I am a good person. I'm a better person than you. You people don't have any right to be tromping around here where my Oliver died."

Suddenly it was quiet. What did she say? Was this the reason Oliver Canfield had her credit card in his office drawer? Could this be the reason she was snooping around the hospital the day we discovered the body? Did Miss Boyle have a boyfriend?

"*My* Oliver?" I asked.

"You heard me. Oliver was mine, and if he hadn't been out here, he never would have died."

"You and Oliver Canfield were ... an item?" asked my dad.

"We were more than 'an item.' We were going to be married." She lifted up her chin with pride, although it wobbled a bit.

"You and Oliver Canfield?" I was amazed. Who knew? It certainly explained a lot, including her mania about keeping us away from the old hospital. If they were choosing this place for a lovers' rendezvous, they sure needed to come up with some better ideas. Why go to this rat hole?

Miss Boyle pulled herself up straight. "Is that so alarming that you think I couldn't attract a man like Oliver?"

We all looked at each other not saying a word. It certainly couldn't be her attitude that attracted him, but it very well could be her credit score.

"He told me that he loved me and couldn't wait to be my husband. We were supposed to get together at four in the afternoon that day, but he never showed up. I knew he had been talking about getting me and ... some others ... together to invest in the hospital, so I figured he was still out here dreaming of our future. He was like that, you know. He was a wonderful man full of ambition. We were going to get married, and then I was going to have a better life than the likes of all of you." She looked straight over at Maggie. "You and your interference." Miss Boyle started screaming. "You killed him!" She lunged after Maggie as my father and Stan pulled her back. "You and your ghosts! You killed him!"

"Leave her alone, you mean lady," Danny yelled. "You leave my mom alone. Go away."

"I'm fine, Danny. It's okay," Maggie reassured him.

"She was going to hurt you." Danny now stood firmly in front of his mother with his hands on his hips.

"No she wasn't. Danny, I'm okay."

"Betsy," my father interrupted. "Do you wish to file charges against Miss Boyle?"

Boy did I ever, but looking at this broken woman, I knew it wouldn't be right. Between the two of us, her with her lonelyhearts con and me with my fretting over being left behind, I was better off. Shaken up a little bit, but at least I wasn't out of my head. "No, I guess not." For the first time in many years, I started feeling like maybe I wasn't the worse sob story in the crowd.

"And then," continued Miss Boyle, seemingly unaware of anyone else, "I discovered Oliver had taken some liberties with my charge card."

"Excuse me?" my father said. Here came the information I truly wanted to hear.

"He ran it up to the limit. But he always said you have to spend money to make money, Bitsy." She smiled. "That's what he called me – Bitsy. Isn't that sweet?"

I recalled that name from his calendar. Miss Boyle was Bitsy? Somehow I had imagined that person just a bit more ... Bitsier.

"He ran through a credit card?" Fitzpatrick said. He was suddenly intensely interested in Miss Boyle's lament. "And he was promising to marry you?"

"We were engaged. I was going to be a Christmas bride," said Miss Boyle.

"It may interest you to know, Miss Boyle, and I'm not saying this to hurt you, Mr. Canfield also proposed to my sister," said Leo Fitzpatrick, stepping forward. Miss Boyle stammered, but Fitzpatrick held up his hand. "And he also used her credit cards and charged them out to the max. I ran a background check on him and found out Oliver Canfield served time. He was in jail for three years for credit card fraud. After he got out, he found his way back to Pecan Bayou and set himself back up in business. He's one of those lonelyhearts Romeos. He's taken lots of women for their money, just like you."

It was then that I saw it. Tyler, who had been standing there quietly, now had tears running down his chubby cheeks. Very quietly, he walked over to Miss Boyle and put his arms around her waist. It was absurd to look at, but then when he spoke it all made sense.

"He was a bad man, Miss Boyle. He hurt my mom, just like you."

Miss Boyle looked down at the boy, and then surprising us all, she put her arms around Tyler to hug him.

Fitzpatrick walked over and tried to unclench Tyler from Miss Boyle. "That's enough, son," he said.

"But Uncle Leo, Mr. Canfield hurt this lady too. Maybe if somebody hugs her and tells her it's all right, she won't ... she won't ..."

"Tyler!"

"Mr. Fitzpatrick," said my father. "Is there something you're not telling us?"

"Tell them, Uncle Leo. We don't have to keep our secret anymore, do we?"

Fitzpatrick gave up trying to separate Tyler from Miss Boyle. Miss Boyle collapsed into Tyler's chubby arms as she fell down on her knees. "I'm so embarrassed. I'm just so embarrassed. I thought he loved me. He just wanted my money." Her emotions were spilling out all over Tyler, who was crying too.

"He made my mama cry too. She went to heaven she was so sad," Tyler said.

"Tyler!"

"Uncle Leo," he said, turning to Fitzpatrick. "This lady was just like mom. If we can't find him, then we can at least help her."

So that was it. Why Leo Fitzpatrick and "son" were actually in town. They came after Canfield, not some pie-in-the-sky investor. Fitzpatrick gave an exasperated sigh and settled down on the bumper next to me.

"Mr. Fitzpatrick, is your son saying you knew Canfield before the murder and that you came to town to seek him out?" asked my dad. Fitzpatrick just shot to number one on the investigation's suspect list.

A cell phone emitted a muffled ring. Benny reached into his pocket and walked away from the Scouts, farther into the woods. Fitzpatrick folded his arms, as we all waited for him to respond. He seemed to be making a decision. He turned to the collapsed form of Maureen Boyle. "Miss Boyle, I know you're hurt, but ... my sister ... she was so devastated by what this man did ... she took her life." He then turned to my father. "And yes, Lieutenant Kelsey, I did come to Pecan Bayou to find Oliver Canfield."

"I think you and I need to have another little talk about the murder of Oliver Canfield."

"I wanted him arrested. I didn't murder him. Whoever did us all that favor wasn't me."

"But you placed yourself at the murder scene. You told me that yourself," I added.

"Yes, I did see Canfield right inside this building." He gestured toward the hospital. "But he was alive. That son-of-a-bitch laughed at me when I told him my sister committed suicide after being a victim of his scam. He laughed and told me that it wasn't his fault my sister, Molly, was so unstable. He started saying stupid things like, 'Ah well, unlucky in love.' I wanted to kill him, but I didn't. I actually left the hospital and was driving to the police station, getting ready to tell everything. It was then I realized I was late picking Tyler up from school. Tyler is my sister's son. She adopted my nephew as a single parent, so when she died I was all the family he had. I was still getting the hang of this whole dad thing and hadn't kept track of the time school ended. As I picked him up, I realized I would be hours at the station and needed to find a babysitter for him. Being so new to town, I had no idea who to call. Instead, I took Tyler out for a hamburger and decided I would go into the sheriff's office the next day. By the time the next day rolled around, it was too late."

"I want to see you in my office first thing in the morning," my dad said. "But not tonight. We're way too busy. Report to my office first thing tomorrow and we'll sort this out."

"But I didn't kill him," Fitzpatrick said.

"We will also open an investigation into the fraud perpetrated against your sister." Tyler had let go of Miss Boyle and was now hugging his uncle.

My dad looked over at the crumpled heap of Miss Boyle. "Ma'am, I want you out of this area and away from my crime scene – right now."

She rose and straightened her gray t-shirt, lifting her head in that now-familiar defiant manner. She cleared her throat as she tried to regain her composure. The weakness in her voice gave her away. "I trust this conversation will remain confidential?"

"Yes, ma'am," my father replied.

"I'm real good at keeping secrets, just ask my Uncle Leo," Tyler added.

She acknowledged him with a slight smile, whispering her response, "Thank you, Tyler. I appreciate that."

Benny ran over to us from the woods. He was out of breath when he reached us. He waved his cell phone in the air as he approached. I could see one of his sons trailing him. "Fitzpatrick, you think you could take over at the campout tonight?"

"Uh, sure. Is something wrong? Are you okay?"

"I'm just fine! Celia just called, and the baby's coming! The labor pains are five minutes apart. I have to get to the house to drive her to the hospital. I think I'm going to have a baby on Halloween!" He gestured back to his campsite. "Benny Jr. will help you out. He's been to a dozen of these things, and if you have any trouble, just call me on my cell."

"I'll be fine. You just go," Fitzpatrick answered.

"Don't worry, Benny," my dad said, "The police will keep an eye on the boys, too." At that, everyone circled around Benny, patting him on the back. He started backing up and waving. We all had a lot on our minds right now, but seeing Benny helped me to remember that my priorities would be with the living, the here and now, not the dead and gone.

As Benny pulled away, Leo Fitzpatrick ran his hand through his hair and put on his ball cap.

"Oh boy. I think this means I'm in charge."

"Ah, nothin' to it," my dad said. "You got the tents up. You just have to get the boys fed and make sure there's enough marshmallows to go around and some sharp sticks to put them on." He patted Leo Fitzpatrick on the back. "Piece-a cake, boy."

He put his hand under Miss Boyle's arm to help her to her car. As they walked away, I could hear my dad talking gently to her as if she hadn't just thwacked his daughter with a water heater.

Danny stepped up to Fitzpatrick. "You want me to help you? I'm real good at helping." Maggie rested her hand on her son's arm. "Danny, I think Mr. Fitzpatrick has enough to deal with."

I wondered what Mr. Fitzpatrick thought about having a mentally disabled person wanting to spend time with him. After all these years growing up with Danny, I knew some people were just fine around him. They didn't seem to care what his IQ score was, and they embraced him for what he was – another human being. Other people became distant from Danny, almost making him feel as if he had done something wrong. He didn't understand that his differences made them uncomfortable.

Barry had been in the second group from the very beginning, even to the point of changing places at a holiday table. He told me that he wanted Danny to be close to his mother so that she could "take care of him." When it came to eating turkey dinners, Danny needed no assistance. It was a lame excuse, and I knew it, but the look on Barry's face, the rigidness of his body, even his tone of voice was painful to watch. Everybody in his world had to fit his own idea of what was normal. Even now I wanted to shake him by the shoulders and tell him his "normal" doesn't exist. The world had two groups. Leo Fitzpatrick was about to prove which one he was in.

"I would love to have the help, Danny," he said with a smile. Danny jumped up and clapped, and the two men headed off towards the woods followed by Tyler and Zach, newfound friends.

"Oooh, I like that fellow, Betsy," Aunt Maggie whispered. Somehow, after all that happened between us, I liked him, too.

CHAPTER EIGHTEEN

THE SUN FINALLY SET, and we worked by the many flashlights we carried around. It was pretty exciting to be actually filming a television program. The ladies from the Best Little Hair House all piled out of Ruby Green's double-cab pickup. Ruby and Anna had their hair freshly sprayed around their paranormal investigator hats. Ruby Green even had her black hair swirled up in the back with a little purple veil decorated with tiny bats, making it look like there were bats flying around her head. I wasn't sure if we were here to find ghosts or aliens, as they resembled a new race of large-headed people invading our planet. Lillian MacPhee had chosen not to embrace the outrageous hairstyle but still sported her paranormal investigator cap on her silver hair. The ladies all set up portable lawn chairs on the edge of the field, and Ruby brought out her cooler stocked with Lone Star beer and margaritas. Maggie promised Howard the celebration would stay at a whisper.

"This is a paranormal investigation, not ladies' night at the bowling alley, Maggie."

"I know," Maggie answered, seeing the cameraman dip in the cooler for a beer. She turned to me, blocking Howard's view.

"Betsy," Maggie said, now holding Howard's clipboard, "are you all set to go down the dead tunnel with me in about an hour's time?"

"Oh Aunt Maggie, maybe Miss Lillian or Miss Ruby would like to go instead." The ladies perked up at that, and Ruby even stood up and adjusted her bat veil, ready for duty. That was fine by me. My mind flashed on how dark it had been in the tunnel in the daytime.

"Did they clear the bats out?"

"They didn't have to. There's a hole in the roof they're flyin' in and out of. Remember, bats are nocturnal, so they're all out huntin' right now. They were pretty harmless, after all."

I remembered pulling one out of my hair, thinking of a scene from the Alfred Hitchcock movie *The Birds*.

"Harmless, huh?"

"Sure, you can do it."

Lillian MacPhee giggled. "Oh, this is so exciting! I don't admit this to a lot of people, but I've watched all the ghost hunting shows they've been showing on TV during Halloween week. It really is fascinating." Seeing her here with Ruby and Anna, Lillian looked much more comfortable than she had been at the council meeting.

Ruby chortled, "Me too!"

Anna hooted, "Me three!"

"Well then I guess that makes you three ladies official members of our little society," Maggie said.

"Aunt Maggie, as one of the founding members, what do you say we send the newbies down the tunnel? It could be an initiation into the group."

Maggie sighed. "You'll be fine, Betsy. I'm goin' down that tunnel, and the only person I want with me is you."

I was touched by her preference for me but still didn't want to go.

Howard was now standing in the main entrance, motioning to me. The cameras were pointing at him, and I was pretty sure they were turned on. Why would he want to talk to me with the cameras on? I don't think I remember Aunt Maggie telling me anything about this.

"Go over there, darlin'," Maggie nudged.

"Me? Why?" I asked, straightening my hair and wondering if I had pulled all the cobwebs out after chasing my intruder down the dusty hallways of the old hospital.

"I don't know what Howard wants, but he needs you on camera, so go, my dear." I trudged over, feeling like an awkward teenager.

"And this evening, we have our resident author and newspaper columnist, The Happy Hinter herself, Betsy Livingston, joining us in the investigation."

I feebly smiled and raised my hand to wave at the camera. Somehow I had achieved "resident celebrity" status.

"What piqued your interest in the paranormal, Betsy?" Howard asked as he handed me the microphone.

"Um, what piqued my interest?" I certainly couldn't tell the truth, that I actually don't have an interest in the paranormal and wasn't even sure if I believed all this hooey. "Well ... I ... guess it runs in the family."

"And that's just wonderful! Betsy is referring to Maggie Schaeffer, one of our esteemed investigators, who is also Betsy's aunt." Howard then nodded toward the building, his grin ever present. "Why don't you go on into the hospital, Betsy, and we'll catch up with you inside." He smiled as his hair picked up a little in the wind. I looked up and saw clouds gathering, covering the moon above us. What else on Halloween? I felt my face muscles start to ache as I forced out one more amicable countenance and waved again.

"Okay Howard, can't wait to see you in there." Boy, did I mean that.

I walked into the now-darkened hospital and immediately over to a small lantern someone had thoughtfully placed inside the door. Once out of the range of the camera, I peered back out through the window. I could see Maggie now being introduced, as she gestured back towards me. The light illuminated the doorways, making them look totally different than they had appeared earlier in the day. I could see the main area and then the six hallways breaking off from them. They had been labeled "A" through "G," and I mentally found Hallway C, which led to the creepy, bat-infested dead tunnel, which led to the morgue. Why couldn't I get the "outside walking" investigation, or better yet, why couldn't I just wait in the van, watching the television transmissions for specters? I heard a chair scrape up on the second floor. I was pretty sure it was George upstairs guarding the crime scene. I heard a faint cough.

"George, are you up there?" I shouted up the stairway to my left.

No answer. "George, are you up there?"

He probably couldn't hear me if he was sitting inside the room.

Maggie showed up at the door. "Ooh-wee, Betsy. This is fun. Once we get all the folks in here we'll sneak back out until it's our time to investigate."

I looked out to see Howard speaking to the ladies from the Hair House. It was gracious of them to put down their alcoholic beverages before going on camera. Howard looked as if he was launching into one of his lectures on the history of the hospital. I turned around to see my Aunt Maggie with her head turned upward, scanning the open area of the ground floor.

"There is something here, Betsy. I can feel it. Do you feel the vibrations?"

I loved my aunt, even in moments like this. Some people see an old dilapidated building, but Maggie saw the history, the toil and the people. She had an open mind and an open heart, and she wasn't afraid to take risks.

At the sound of footsteps, I turned around expecting to see the ladies coming through the door, but instead, Danny nearly knocked me over. He was breathing heavily.

"Betsy, Mama ... Mr. Leo sent me over here. He wants to know if you've seen Tyler or Zach." He put his hands on his knees, gasping for breath.

"No," I answered. "I thought they were over there with you."

He looked towards his feet, still trying to regulate his breathing. "I wasn't a good helper."

Maggie put her arm around her son. "Sure you were. What happened?"

"Mr. Leo told me to go get them – Zach and that Tyler boy – to help pull logs around for seats at the roaring fire. I went to their tent, but they weren't there. I lost them."

"Are you sure? Maybe they were in another tent with some of the other Scouts? Maybe they went out in the woods to use the restroom?" I said.

"No, I looked in all the tents, and Zach and that Tyler boy weren't there. They weren't anywhere, and it's all my fault."

"Well, that wasn't your fault."

"I lost Zach." His eyes, illuminated by the shadows of the lantern, seemed to be framed by the jutting of his cheekbones. He ran his hands through his straight, thin hair and started repeating, "It's my fault. It's my fault."

"Do you want to be a good helper now?" Maggie cut in. "Go look and see if Uncle Judd's police car is out there and tell him Zach and Tyler are lost and that we need to all search for them. Tell Mr. Leo we will start looking for the boys over here. Okay?"

"Okay," he answered.

"Repeat it for me," said Maggie.

"Go find Uncle Judd. Go tell Mr. Leo." He echoed the phrase as he ran out the door, nearly knocking over Ruby and company as they entered, tittering about their onscreen interviews.

"Sorry, Miss Ruby," he shouted as he ran down the stairway to the outdoors.

"Ladies, we have two boys missing," Aunt Maggie said in her no-nonsense voice. The ladies gasped. Aunt Maggie started informing her posse as to details and search patterns.

"Where would they have gone to, Betsy?" Maggie asked.

I kicked at a stray piece of paper as I opened my cell phone to call my dad. "I don't know. I don't know whether to be mad or worried."

"First find them and then decide, darlin'."

I agreed and then listened to my dad's voicemail click on.

Within a few minutes, Leo Fitzpatrick showed up, looking as if he had run the entire way. I noticed there was now a slight breeze, and I could hear some rumbling in the distance. I glanced out the window. A patch of clouds drifted across a full moon. I could smell the moisture in the air, hinting at a cooling rain. Maggie had deputized the Hair House ladies and assigned them each a hallway on the main floor, taking one herself. They walked through the hospital, bouffant hair bobbing, calling out the boys' names.

"I left Danny in charge with all the Scouts sitting around the fire. Benny's sons were helping out, too. They were going to sing camp songs to keep them busy," said Fitzpatrick.

"Good," my father said as he stepped through the doorway. "I hope they know a lot of them."

I felt relief flooding through me. He had gotten my voicemail. He took off his Stetson and ambled over to me.

Leo continued, "Betsy, do you think the boys might have come over here?"

"I don't know what for." I felt my insides freezing up. Would I lose Zach as well as Barry? Here one day, gone the next? Had the fates actually planned a giant zinger my way once more? The panic set in, and I could barely hear for the blood rushing inside my head.

Fitzpatrick shrugged. "The boys seemed to be getting along really well. I think they were talking about Tyler's mom and

Zach's dad. Tyler even apologized about saying your husband was the dead body you found here."

Tyler was right. Canfield did link back to my missing husband. Finding him brought back so many memories of Barry. A thought thundered into my mind. My dad put his Stetson back on, and it seemed he had the same thought. I grabbed the lantern, and we both ran for the stairs. As the rest of the group all clambered behind us, I saw a giant man standing at the top of the stairs holding a tiny deputy and a slightly chubby pirate by the collar.

"Hey there, Judd, look who I found wanderin' around our crime scene." George Beckman's high voice echoed across the empty lobby. Both boys wriggled out from his grasp and ran down the stairs.

"What in the hell were you two doing up there?" My father stood with both his hands on his gun belt.

"We were investigating," Zach said matter-of-factly.

"I think we are knee-deep in so-called investigators tonight, boy."

Tyler, who had been unusually subdued, spoke quietly to my dad. "We were looking for Zach's dad."

We could still hear the Hair House ladies calling up and down the hallways. "Miss Ruby, Miss Lillian, Miss Anna, Miss Maggie, we found 'em," George yelled out, his voice echoing through the corridors.

I went over to Zach and knelt down to come face-to-face with him. Fitzpatrick remained standing, his arms crossed and his attitude stern.

"Why were you looking for Barry up there?" I asked, although I was already starting to understand my son's motives.

"Because ... well ... Tyler and I were talking about it and ... and ... well ... maybe Dad was there. Maybe he and Mr. Canfield were still partners and working together."

I took his small hands in my own. "Listen to me. Your dad was not up there. We do not know where your dad is. We don't know if he was the victim of a crime of any type, but we're pretty sure he wasn't. We believe that he ... just left." Zach looked down, trying shut out my last statement.

"He just left," I repeated. "He left the best little boy God ever made, and for that he has lost an incredible treasure – you. I'm sorry he's not here with you tonight or tomorrow and a thousand tomorrows, but I am here, and I always will be." Zach's little arms encircled my neck, cast and all, in the kind of neck-breaking hug only a kid can give.

"And I am too, sport," my father whispered, now standing behind us joining into the embrace.

"Are we in trouble?" asked Tyler.

"Yes," Fitzpatrick answered. Tyler started to get his now familiar scowl. His uncle continued, "But ... I guess you had your reasons." Tyler's shock registered, and then he ran down the remaining stairs to Leo.

"It was real scary up there, Uncle Leo. I'm glad you found us."

"I know," he said as he tousled his nephew's hair affectionately. "I'm glad I found you, too."

Somehow I felt he was not just talking about the crime scene incident.

A light started sneaking in from around the corner, and I realized the film crew was now moving with Howard into the hospital.

"And now we enter the fabled Johnson Tuberculosis Hospital." Howard came around the corner with portable lights held up by the crew trailing him. His voice reminded me of a late-show announcer on the creature feature movie. His back was to us as he walked facing the camera. "Be on the lookout for apparitions, black shadows lingering in a room and poltergeists."

"Boo!" squeaked George Beckman at the top of the stairs. Howard jumped, emitting a scream as he ran back out the door. The whole group gathered at the stairs exploded in laughter.

CHAPTER NINETEEN

AN HOUR LATER, AS WE watched Howard on the television monitor, all of the emotions of the afternoon seemed to be haunting me. Leo really wasn't a dad, but he was a decent enough brother to come to town to fight for his sister. Tyler wasn't his son, after all. It was a lot to take in about him. The fact that he was single and not one of the many walking wounded from the relationship wars made him more appealing as well. For the first time in a long time, I started thinking of myself no longer in a one-person marriage with Barry, but as a single woman. I thought about those blue eyes peering into me, sharing his water on the back step of the hospital, and the way he came to the aid of my own son. This could be a beginning and the kind of dream I hadn't allowed myself in a long while. Whose fault was that, really? I could have come out of my self-imposed fog years ago, but, like Miss Boyle, I was tortured by my trap.

Stanley came over, pulling earphones from his ears. "Betsy, after Howard finishes this part, we're moving on to the walk you and Maggie are taking next. I need you to stay here near the van until we're ready for you."

"Okay," I answered. I looked around for Maggie. She had been passing out cups of coffee about a half-hour ago. We returned the boys to the campsite and had finally settled down to some ghost hunting. I walked over to the van area, where I joined the Hair House Ladies but passed on the refreshments from their cooler. I sat down on the grass and leaned up against the wheel of the van.

I yawned as the long day was beginning to catch up with me. I now knew who one of the people on Canfield's calendar was. I also knew he met up with Fitzpatrick but still didn't know who Roy was. I searched my memory trying to single out anyone with that name in this town. It reminded me of old cowboy movies. And then there was the question of the concrete. Why did Canfield have fresh concrete on him? Had he just put in a sidewalk? Had he just buried someone and put a concrete slab on the top? Why, of all places, was he stuffed into a hole in the wall and left there? Who would know that such a thing existed?

Stanley walked back over and sat down on the ground next to me. He bumped back his baseball cap, going for the "Ron Howard on a big film shoot" look. "So Betsy, I've been reading your Happy Hinter column in the paper every week. Very helpful stuff."

Oh, maybe someone else was going to hire me to do an efficiency evaluation. Looked like my Christmas fund was about to get a boost.

"I was wondering if you would be interested in doing a little fifteen-minute segment each week giving helpful hints to our viewers?"

"Really?" I wasn't expecting that. I spent the last seven years avoiding the community at large, and now they wanted me in each and every living room once a week? That was wild.

"Uh, I don't know Stanley. I'm ... uh ... pretty busy with keeping up with my columns." I stalled. I wasn't quite sure how comfortable I was with the idea of being on television, even if it was cable access, which meant the viewing numbers were somewhat smaller than the local Elks meeting. "Let me think about it."

"Sure. I understand. You probably don't know this about me, but I read all your columns." He smiled, a little embarrassed. "I'm a bit of a homebody at heart. Great hint about separating egg whites from yolks only when they're very cold, by the way. I finally made the perfect meringue."

"That's good to hear. Did you stay away from mixing it in a plastic bowl?"

Stanley saluted, tapping his ball cap. "Metal or glass, just like you said."

"Glad I could be of help," I answered. It might not be all that terrible being on NUTV, I thought. "I'll let you know." I was getting stiff from sitting on the ground and stood up to stretch. "Let me go find Maggie. I think I saw her go around the corner. I know she won't want to miss this."

I walked off into the darkness, clicking on my flashlight as I thought about Stanley's request. Could I actually fill up fifteen minutes of airtime once a week? It would mean more income for me and Zach, but it would also mean having to get out of my pajamas and show up somewhere every week. So much to think about.

I looked around the back of the NUTV van but didn't see Maggie. Maybe she went back to the car to get something. I walked through the overgrown grass trying not to think of all the creatures that crawl out at night. She could have also been catching a little catnap. She wasn't exactly a spring chicken, and we were way past her bedtime.

"Aunt Maggie?" I called out. My voice sounded small in the expanse of the night. "Aunt Maggie, are you in here?" I shined my light into the car, but the car was empty. Maggie wasn't there.

I turned around and searched across the grass with my flashlight. I could see the fire at the Scout camp but couldn't see my aunt sitting on any of the stumps around it. I walked to the edge of the woods close to where my little deputy was sitting by Tyler at the fire. I called over to him. "Zach? Have you seen Aunt Maggie?"

Zach turned toward my voice. "Mom? Is that you?" He scrambled up from his seat by the fire and ran over with Tyler behind him.

"Yes, it's me. Did Aunt Maggie come over?"

"Nope. We haven't seen her since we left the haunted hospital." Zach nodded and smiled. He was no doubt a legend with the Scouts now that he had entered a haunted place and penetrated a crime scene, all at the age of seven. They were probably building a statue of him out of Popsicle sticks at this very moment.

I sighed. Aunt Maggie wouldn't be happy if she missed her chance to mingle with the spirits on camera. Besides, I wasn't going on a walk down those hallways by myself that was for sure.

Tyler jumped in. "Do you need us to help look for her? We are Scouts, ma'am, and trained to do this sort of thing."

Only because their members keep getting themselves lost, I thought.

"No, I'll find her, but thanks," I answered.

I trudged back to the "haunted hospital." Stanley walked part of the way toward me.

"Any luck?" he asked.

"No, and she wasn't over at the Scout camp."

"Okay. Let's check and see if she's gone into the front part of the building. Maybe she was checking out some of the areas you were going to be walking in."

"Where was that exactly going to be again?"

Stanley looked at a clipboard by the monitor. "Hallway C and the tunnel to the morgue."

I knew it. "I thought Howard was going to do that one."

"Yes, well he was originally slated to do it, but I switched it to you and Maggie. I wanted the best screamers in the dead tunnel."

Somehow I wasn't in the mood to appreciate his humor. "Great."

"Howard just finished his segment. Let's take a break on the filming and spread out to look for her. I'll get Miss Ruby and the ladies to look on the other side. I bet they had no idea they would spend their night searching for lost people who were alive," Stanley said.

A few minutes later, I was inside the hospital with my flashlight as my only companion. Howard went upstairs to see if Maggie was revisiting the crime scene, and I was walking through our assigned path, Hallway C and the dead tunnel.

During the day, this hallway seemed much shorter and fairly safe. Now, at night, every piece of peeling paint, every door hanging by one hinge, every shuffle of my feet seemed amplified. "Aunt Maggie?" How could it get so dark in one place? Somehow it had become darker than black. "Aunt Maggie?"

I started down Hallway C with a half-dozen doorways on each side of me. What if she had been walking around and tripped over some debris and hit her head? She could have gone into one of these rooms searching out some sort of flickering orb or shadow, tripped over an old ceiling tile and hit the floor. There were still some pieces of rusty and broken furniture in many of these rooms that she could have fallen into. My mind started racing as I shined my flashlight at the door immediately to my right. If something dreadful was in here, if there was something otherworldly, it could jump out at me from any of these doors. Suddenly I wished my aunt had asked me to help her with a regular old-lady hobby like sewing a quilt top or planting a prize-winning rose garden. But no, my aunt had to go off ghost-chasing. My aunt had to risk both her body and soul to this crazy idea.

I took one step forward, and then way down the hall I thought I heard something. Had I heard the guttural sound of a throat clearing? "Aunt Maggie? Is that you? Are you all right?"

I took another step and shined my light into the empty room, with the handgun-bearing reflexes of a television cop. I scanned the room, only to be greeted by empty windows and part of a bed frame. No one was there. I walked over to the closet, its door hanging sideways. Also empty. I backed out just in case the ghosts that weren't there were keen to jump me. I flicked my light to the other room on the other side of the hall and all I saw was an old curtain hanging from the window, stirring slightly with an evening breeze. Normally I would be through the roof to feel a breeze, but right now I felt a set of goose bumps uncomfortably spread under my skin.

I heard a shifting further down the hall, and then full-on footsteps. There was a raspy noise that rattled me. What was this? I seemed to be spending all my time chasing after someone I had never seen running through this hospital. The term "wild goose chase" was flashing through my head as I picked up my feet. I ignored the pounding in my heart and high-tailed it down the hall. I just had to hope against hope nothing popped out at me like a five-dollar haunted house visit on Halloween.

I ran down the hallway yelling, "Aunt Maggie? What is going on?" I turned the corner of the hallway, glad for once I didn't hear the footsteps take the stairs, although running into Howard upstairs would have done a lot for my nerves right now. My flashlight beam now bounced against the walls as I ran, making shadows sway with each move. Who needed a fake haunted house when we were live at the haunted hospital, right here? The footsteps continued in front of me until I came face-to-face with one of the few closed doors in the whole joint. It was the door to the morgue. It seemed large and imposing, quietly wait for me at the end of the hallway. I stepped back from it.

"Howard? Can you hear me? Stanley? Ruby? Ladies?" I wanted anybody in hearing range. I could faintly hear Maggie's name being called throughout the hospital, but they couldn't seem to hear me. As crazy as Maggie was about ghost hunting, I couldn't believe she would go down the dead tunnel by herself.

Even with the bats gone, there was no way I was going down this tunnel by myself. I scanned the area again with my flashlight. Maybe I could still get a volunteer to go with me. As I shined the light on the floor about three feet from the door, up against the wall, I could see a small black rectangular box. It was a walkie-talkie like the ones I had seen Stanley and Howard using. I grabbed for it.

"Howard? Are you there?"

I was greeted with static and some indistinct voices. The red light that came on when I pushed the button grew more and more faint with every button push. The batteries were dying. I was about to turn around and physically go find Howard or Stanley to go down the tunnel with me when I heard it. A thin, piercing wail that I knew instinctively – I heard Aunt Maggie scream.

It was time to go down the dead tunnel.

CHAPTER TWENTY

AUNT MAGGIE'S VOICE cut through the night. I felt panic rising up inside me. I tried the walkie-talkie again.

"Howard? Stanley? Ruby?" I shouted into the walkie-talkie. "If anyone out there can hear me, Maggie is in trouble. We are at the dead tunnel." I got only weak static in reply. I clipped the walkie-talkie to my belt and held my breath. Hopefully the bats had gone out for the evening. If not, I would have to run through them. I pulled open the door, half expecting the mob of bats to be still waiting there, ready to pounce. I waited for the assault, for the hundreds of little wings, feet and tiny teeth on my face and in my hair. I was greeted instead with a black, cold stillness. The bats seemed to be gone.

Like so much of my life, here I was alone again with an extremely dark expanse in front of me. I don't know why I kept getting myself in this situation. Clearly I was no good at it. The most important thing here was not my fear, it was Maggie. My dear, dear Maggie. Was she hurt? Was she in trouble? Did she fall and break a hip? Fear or no fear, I had to find her.

"Aunt Maggie? Are you down there?" Down there, at the end of all this darkness, this concrete tunnel with no windows.

I felt as if I was being swallowed up. I was going down this giant concrete conduit straight to hell.

"Aunt Maggie? Can you hear me?"

It was quiet now. No footsteps, no screams, just me and my fears. I knew I had to move forward, no matter what. I remembered I had a cell phone in my pocket, so I pulled it out to call my dad and as many people that I could think of representing law enforcement in this town. I flipped open the comforting light of the phone to find I had no bars. I took a step forward. This time I couldn't shrink back. I couldn't call my dad. I couldn't even choose not to.

"Aunt Maggie, I'm coming," I yelled and took off running down the pitch-black tube. There would not be one more body in this dead tunnel. My feet slapped on the concrete as I began to see a faint light. I was running fast now as I yelled out her name. I was the bullet soaring down the chamber. I was moving at such speed, I was knocked back by the sudden impact of a face staring into mine.

It looked red and somehow disfigured, with eyes too bright, staring out at me.

It was the face of Dr. MacPhee.

"Dr. Mac!" I fell into his arms. I was relieved to see him but was unsure as to why he looked so strange.

"Thank God you're here." I ran through my words gasping for breath. "I think my Aunt Maggie's in trouble."

"I think she is, too." His answer was strangely calm. He tightened his grip on my arms and propelled me through the door and onto the floor of the morgue. As I went down, I felt something hard and cushy all at the same time. From the moan I heard, I knew I had just landed on Aunt Maggie.

"Unbelievable, you people. You just had to pursue this, didn't you?"

"Dr. Mac?"

"Dr. Mac?" He mocked me using a falsetto. "Oh, Dr. Mac can't you help my dear old Auntie? She wants to do this half-assed ghost hunt in the old hospital. Oh, Mac, you've always been there for me."

Aunt Maggie stirred beside me. I could see a gash on her head. There was a battery-powered lantern glowing on the far side of the room. The beige ceramic tiles that lined the wall shone in the glow of it. I could imagine many years ago this being a clean and glistening place instead of the dusty bat-filled haven it had become. There was a hole in the roof where the bats had made their entrances and exits over the years. In the corner of the room, there was a square metal box rusted with age. It reminded me of the pizza oven down at Dominic's Flying Pizza in town. There was one door that hung precariously on what was left of a hinge. It had to weigh fifty pounds, judging by the thickness of the metal. Inside was what looked like a concrete mass with what I was sure was a skeletal hand and arm sticking out of it. It was as if the skeleton were reaching out toward anyone walking by. When I looked back at Dr. Mac, I could see he was holding a Colt .45 automatic and pointing it right at us. Being the daughter of a policeman, I instantly recognized the pistol with the black, boxy shape.

"People in this God-forsaken town are way too nosy. Bunch of whiners," Dr. Mac continued his high falsetto as he mimicked his patients. "Help me doctor, I can't pay you. Help me doctor, my husband left me." He walked over to the metal box with the bony hand reaching towards him.

"This little gal here was a whiner. Let me formally introduce you to Mrs. Vickie MacPhee, my first wife. She hailed from the great state of Mississippi. She was dirt poor, white trash, came from a town called Farley's Ditch. That's right, a town named after a ditch. She came from the kind of people nobody takes notice of or particularly cares about. Did you know that after I killed her, not a soul, not a single solitary person came looking for her? Not one. She's a throwaway, so I threw her. You see, I was an orderly out here at the hospital. Back then I called myself Roy."

"I was fresh out of the service and always looking for an angle to get out of being the poor country bumpkin that I was. I thought I hit pay dirt when I found a young lady on the hospital ward with the last name DuPont. As in the DuPont family of enormous wealth? Everyone knew the DuPonts were loaded, and here I had found one lonely, quite unattractive DuPont looking for her knight in shining armor. Sadly, it seemed her family didn't have much to do with Miss Vickie, so I swooped in to rescue her. I courted her for one week and then announced I was so hopelessly in love I wanted to marry her. My, my, but she was taken aback. Who would have thought here she was confronting death, and she gets a marriage proposal? Back then, I was afraid I would spoil everything if I asked her just exactly what her bank balance was. It was a life lesson, you could say. It wasn't until after I married her that I found out she was just another disgustingly poor person like me."

"And then, miracle of miracles she got cured. Cured! She couldn't even afford to pay her own hospital bill. I moved her into my apartment and continued working out at the hospital until it closed. I hated her. I hated everything about her. After the hospital, I got a job out at the local country club where I met my present wife, Lillian. Her maiden name was Lillian Chambers. Doesn't that just drip with money? This time I checked her out and found out her daddy was one of the richest men in Pecan Bayou. Luckily, her daddy didn't return the favor and check me out in reverse. I told her that I was a struggling college student between scholarships and that above all else I wanted to go to medical school."

"My only problem was I had to do something with Vickie here. It was so easy, you wouldn't believe it. Her energy level never truly returned after her illness, so I told her that she had to have a daily hot toddy with a dash of liquid vitamin stirred in. Actually, she only needed one. The one I filled with cyanide. Did you know she smiled at me as I handed her that steaming cup of poison? Trusting until the end, dumb bitch. After she died, I brought her out here to the cooler in the morgue. The tuberculosis hospital didn't keep bodies for long, maybe a day or two, but then they sent them off elsewhere. They kept them in this cooling unit. I put a lock on the door and got the hell out of here. I always meant to come back, but to tell the truth, it all unnerved me a bit. Every cadaver I operated on in medical school made me think of her, decomposing and stinking out here. I couldn't make myself come back, no matter how hard I tried. I just hoped that someday they would bulldoze the building and her with it. I filed for a divorce on the grounds of abandonment, and then a year later I married Lillian."

"Her daddy wasn't that keen on me until he knew I was a potential doctor for his sacred family tree. That old fool not only let me marry his daughter, but he paid for medical school."

Dr. Mac walked over to the square box containing the body of his wife encased in the crumbling concrete. "It sealed up so tightly, even with the electricity not running. I felt sure someone would find her, year after year after year, but strangely no one did. It really was as if she was an invisible person. Frankly, there were times when I actually forgot about her being out here. No one came looking for her, and no one ever found her body. No one, that is, until Oliver Canfield."

I looked over at Aunt Maggie, whose eyes were now open. She didn't stir but sat quietly, listening to the unraveling of many years of deceit.

"What a piece of work that one was," Dr. Mac continued. "He was nosing around out here and actually pried off the door to the cooler. When what to his wondering eyes should appear," he shook his head to emphasize each word, "but my dear ol' Vickie here. Surprise!" He jumped at me as if he were a crazed birthday clown. "I'll say one thing for that Canfield guy – he was clever, very clever. He just wasn't as clever as I was. This is a man's game, and he was a mere boy. He thought he had one up on me because he took the wedding band off her finger. Inside was inscribed Love, Roy. I don't go by that name anymore. It's a country-sounding name, don't you think?"

I nodded dumbly.

"Yes. You see, here I go by Dr. William R. MacPhee. It sounds much better, doesn't it? It seems Canfield had done title searches on several pieces of property here in town, and from that he picked up on my middle name. He took that ring from her bony finger and put it on his fat little finger. I don't know how he got it on there. I had to use oil from the gun to pull it off of him. Of course, he was dead by then, so he didn't struggle much. He asked to meet me, right here in this hospital. But I guess you know that part because you found him!" He laughed at his own joke.

"He knew I killed her, but that was when I was a young fellow. I mean, look at me. I'm an old man who delivers babies and puts casts on little leaguers. What a sweet old guy I turned out to be! I simply walked through the woods from the hospital while the nurses thought I was taking a short nap. They wouldn't dare disturb me, dear old Dr. Mac. I hid the gun in my belt, under my jacket. I told Canfield to meet me in Room 227, knowing about the hole in the wall. We used to joke that was the real employee's lounge. We could hide out there and avoid changing bedpans and helping all the coughing, weak people stretching out their hands to us. They were disgusting, always retching up bile." He grimaced.

"So Canfield walks up to me, spouting all of this rubbish about how he knows I killed my wife but I could pay him a million dollars and he'd forget all about it. I just couldn't let that happen, you see. I had created this perfect life and had put Vickie way, way behind me. He was quite surprised when I pulled my Colt out of my jacket. I shot him, and then the son-of-a-bitch laughed at me. He tells me that I'll never get her out. He encased her in concrete. It was his guarantee she would stay right here. I shot him again and stuffed him in the wall, and even though I hated the thought, I ran down to the morgue and found my Vickie settled into a bed of concrete. Canfield had outsmarted me."

"Were you the one who set the fire at Canfield's office?" I asked.

"You are way too nosy. Just like the rest of this town. You see, Canfield might have left some sort of connection to me at his office. I was about to start a fire, but then I saw you sneaking up the stairs. If you had found something, then you would have to be taken care of as well. I hit you with some outlandish-looking cowboy statue and was getting ready to hit you again when I saw someone else coming up the stairs. I stepped back and hid behind a filing cabinet while Mr. Fitzpatrick dragged you out through the fire. I barely made it out myself, but luckily the two of you never looked back as I ran out of the building."

"So Fitzpatrick had nothing to do with it?"

"No, my dear. He seemed to be there to look after you, not hurt you."

I felt warmed by that, though still wondering if he had been following me.

"I knew I couldn't return here because of the guard your father posted. Tonight, I knew you would come into this room, so I decided one last time to try and dig out Vickie. I was making headway until your aunt showed up. "

MacPhee looked lovingly at his handgun. He caressed the top. "I used this old gun in Vietnam, and now it continues to protect and serve. And now it will do its job for me again."

He glanced down at Maggie, and his face took on a wicked grin.

"Ahh, the ghost of the Johnson TB Hospital ... ahhhh!" He swirled around with his arms out, imitating an exceedingly bad ghost. He turned first one way and then the next. It was on the second turn that I stuck my foot out and tripped him. He fell backwards but kept hold of the gun, shooting one bullet into the ceiling. I went over and grabbed the cooler door and with all my strength attempted to clobber Dr. Mac on the head with it. As it came down I heard the thundering noise of another bullet, this time aimed right at me. I shut my eyes and put all of my strength into swinging the door. I heard something shoot past my ear as we both landed on the ground in a sort of grotesque human sandwich. Dr. Mac groaned and then became still.

The door to the morgue burst open and Howard came in, trying to threaten a killer with his flashlight. My father came in behind him, gun drawn and shouting. I had never been so happy to see him.

AN HOUR LATER, I STOOD out by the police cruiser with Zach holding onto my waist. All of the Scouts were running around now, while Leo and Danny were trying to corral them back to the woods.

"Are you sure you're all right, Mom?"

"I'm fine. It's Aunt Maggie you need to worry about."

My dad pushed the hair back from his grandson's forehead. "The paramedics said that she has a nasty cut on her head but that she will be fine. They just took her over to the hospital to check her out. After I ask a few more questions, you two can go over to the hospital to see her." He looked a little tired tonight. A little grayer, and at least one more wrinkle had formed at his brow. Nobody ever said living with our family was easy.

"I can't believe what just happened." I shook my head.

"Well, you saved her, baby girl. I couldn't believe it when I ran with in with Howard and there you were with that man squished under that door. I've never been much for religion, but at that moment, I shot up a prayer of thanks to the Almighty."

Leo Fitzpatrick walked up. "Mrs. Livingston, you and your family certainly seem to have a need for a full-time paramedic crew." I laughed.

He continued, "I'm just glad you and your aunt are okay. Did I hear you dodged a bullet?"

"She sure did. He shot at her, and it went straight through the cooler door and past her ear."

"Wow," said Zach. His mom just rose on the cool scale.

"Just like the bad guys on the TV," Danny agreed.

"I just can't believe he killed Canfield. I always thought he was the kindest man in town. I told him everything over the years," I said.

Miss Ruby came around the corner, her arm guiding Lillian MacPhee. She had taken her cap off and was shaking. She looked over to me. "What have you done to my husband?" She spoke in a tinny voice that was almost too soft to hear.

My father stepped in front of me. "Your husband is on his way to the police station. He has been arrested for attempted murder and has confessed to killing his first wife, and confessed to the murder of Oliver Canfield."

That knocked the wind right out of her. Confusion spread over her face. "You're wrong. I am his first wife, and I am most definitely alive."

"Lillian," said Miss Ruby, "what do you say I drive you down to the police station? Would that be good?"

Miss Lillian stepped away from her. Her voice became shrill. "Why did you hurt my husband? Whatever did he do to you? Why are you so ungrateful after he's worked for so many years tending to your family? Doesn't that mean anything to you?"

I know I should have been kind and understanding at this point because she was about to learn a whole lot about her husband, but her voice had taken on a haughty tone.

"Yes, well he pointed a gun at me, and I'm pretty sure he meant to kill me when he shot it at me."

"I don't know why you are lying about William, but you can bet our family lawyer will be in touch." With that, she returned to Miss Ruby, and they headed for her pickup truck.

CHAPTER TWENTY-ONE

ON THE FOLLOWING MONDAY evening, Zach and I pulled up to Benny's Barbecue just as he was taking the skeleton out of the window and replacing it with a fluffy brown-and-orange paper turkey. We ran inside through falling rain. The temperature had dropped about twenty degrees since the campout as a cold front moved through Texas. The long, never-ending summer had finally ended. The rain refreshed my soul as I pulled up the hood of my raincoat.

Inside, we were met by Maggie, Danny, Dad, Stanley from NUTV, Howard, Tyler and Leo Fitzpatrick. Benny pushed two tables together, and we all talked and laughed like a family on a holiday. The mood continued when Celia came in with her and Benny's new baby girl, Mia.

"She is beautiful," I said as she grabbed my little finger with her hand.

"Yes, she is," Celia said. "I finally have me a little girl. Sugar and spice – and I don't want to see her daddy signing her up for that Scout troop." She laughed.

"Yes, ma'am." Benny nodded obediently.

"I'm just so glad things are returning to normal, although I am going to have to find a new family doctor for us," I said.

"So you were the one who figured out that MacPhee pulled a ring off of Canfield's finger," Fitzpatrick said.

"Yes, I figured that part out, but when I found the name 'Roy' on Canfield's calendar, I was stumped."

My father added, "The 'Roy' was MacPhee, the sleazy orderly, before he reinvented himself into the lovable town doctor. That was one reason he knew just how to deal with Canfield. It takes a con to know a con."

"How is Miss Lillian doing?" I asked.

"She's been down at the station with her lawyer, visiting with Dr. MacPhee pretty damn near all weekend. I think she's starting to recognize her husband for what he really is. When all this comes to light she just might be usin' that lawyer for a good ol' Texas divorce."

I turned to Leo Fitzpatrick. "So are you returning to Dallas now?"

"Yes, I guess so. I guess you should know I don't work for an investment firm. Actually, I'm a meteorologist, but after my sister ... well ... I took a leave of absence to take time with Tyler. At first we were just going to be getting used to living together, but when I found Oliver Canfield's address among my sister's things, I just had to come down here and find him. I didn't know what I was going to do, but I was going to do something."

"Hmm, a meteorologist in Texas. I'll bet you're plenty busy watching all the big hurricanes," I said.

"Yes, but I think my little visit to Pecan Bayou has shown me there's some pretty decent weather outside of the Big D." His eyes searched me out, and I had the feeling I was being looked at like a fine swirling funnel cloud.

"Well, we're all glad you and Tyler came, no matter what the reason."

"Maybe, before we leave, I can return the favor of the wonderful dinner you made for us."

I blushed. "That would be great." I couldn't believe I just said yes to a date. This was my week for significant changes, it seemed. I looked over at Zach, who nodded his approval.

"You know, I just wish my sister was here to see all this," Fitzpatrick said.

Maggie put her hand on Fitzpatrick's arm. "She's here, Leo. She's here, and she's proud to know that Tyler is being raised by such a strong man."

Leo Fitzpatrick gave my aunt a soft grin as his eyes rimmed with tears. He looked away, embarrassed by his show of emotion. Maggie continued, moving the topic tactfully away from his sister.

"I can't believe how cold Dr. MacPhee became. He seemed like such a lovely man when you were in the hospital with Zach."

"It was all an act, I guess," I said.

Benny walked over with a plate of beignets. "An act Canfield saw through. What's that saying – you can't kid a kidder? Canfield figured out his weakness and was ready to add him to his list of suckers."

Fitzpatrick took a light, delicious pastry from the tray. "Yeah, I heard what he was doing to you and your business."

"Things are still tough for us," Benny said, "but at least he has his hooks out of me now."

"That reminds me," Stanley said, rubbing the powdered sugar off his hands. "We were wondering if you would consider bringing some barbecue plates out for our crews when we film the turkey shoot in a couple of weeks. Perhaps we could trade for some free advertising? I don't mean to brag, but I can put together a pretty good commercial."

Benny smiled, rubbed his hands on his apron and grabbed Stanley's hand. "You've got a deal."

Maggie sighed. "I just wish we would have seen a ghost. Just one single little apparition."

"Aunt Maggie, with all that was going on, I don't even think we got enough footage for the program," I said.

"Oh! I forgot." Stanley rummaged in his pocket and brought out his phone. "I brought some footage of the program we uploaded. I put the video on my phone because it was so amazing. We had one shot of Betsy walking into the hospital when we were testing the thermal camera, and it was just incredible."

I remembered the thermal camera was a device that shot film in bright yellow and orange. It looked like a Peter Maxx painting with layers and layers of color around its subjects, picking up on their heat patterns. Stanley started the video on his phone. I could see myself walking into the hospital carrying one of the recording cases. The camera followed me, and as I stepped onto the front stoop and looked back, there it was, clear as a bell, a deep red wisp of a thing that seemed to be following me. It darted around a couple of times, reminding me of Zach when he wanted something from me. It seemed to be trying to get my attention. I, of course, was clueless to its existence.

"Oh my word," Aunt Maggie said. "Betsy, you have a spirit. You have an apparition following you."

"I need to confess something," I said. "I have never really believed in ghosts."

Aunt Maggie gasped.

"But I felt like there was someone around me the whole time. I kept hearing those footsteps, and this is really going to sound silly, but whoever it was must have had a chest cold. I kept hearing coughing."

"I know who it was," said Howard as he stared at Stanley's phone.

"You know the name of this ghost?" This was going to be good, I thought.

"It was Vickie."

"Vickie MacPhee?"

"She was trying to lead you to her body."

Cue the Twilight Zone music. Too weird. "Me? Of all the people out there, Howard, why would she choose me? Why not you with your paranormal degree? I was just an unwilling extra who was signed on to help. That doesn't make any sense."

"You were like her," Maggie said. She looked up at me, her blue eyes seeing into my soul. "Don't you see? She saw in you things that were in herself. She was alone. You were alone. She was duped by the man she loved, and you were the same. She sensed in you a sister in her despair, and in the end, you were the one who freed her from her prison."

I ran my hands through my hair, drawing in a breath. Was that true? Was I as pitiful a person as the dead Vickie DuPont MacPhee? In one part of my brain I knew she was right, but in another, I knew it didn't have to be that way. I had so many things Vickie didn't have. I had a child I loved dearly, as well as a family I couldn't live without. My family would never leave me to rot in a hospital like Vickie's did. I had a career, and even if there wasn't always a man in the picture, that was okay, too.

Yes, I had a much better life than Vickie MacPhee, and from here on out I knew it would get better. Instead of waiting like she did, year after year in the old hospital, I was now living my life in the present and maybe a little in the future. Life was about what was happening today, not about what happened way in the past. Barry had been mixed up with Oliver Canfield, and now Canfield was dead. Was Barry dead? I still didn't know. I don't know if I ever will.

"Betsy?" my aunt said. "A penny for your thoughts? Are we sunshine or shadows?"

"Sunshine, Aunt Maggie, all sunshine," I answered.

HELPFUL HINTS FROM THE HAPPY HINTER

BENNY'S BBQ SAUCE

    1/4 cup cider vinegar

    1/2 cup ketchup

    1/2 cup water

    3 tablespoons brown sugar

    1 teaspoon salt

    1 teaspoon chili powder

Directions

In a medium bowl or bottle, combine the vinegar, ketchup, water, brown sugar, salt and chili powder. Mix well and store in the refrigerator until ready for use.

How to Get a Stuck Ring off Your Finger

Put your hand in a bowl of ice water until the finger contracts enough to remove the ring.

You may also want to ice your hand and raise it above your heart for about ten to fifteen minutes. Then massage your finger, pushing towards your hand.

Ten Ways to Stay Safe in the Heat

1. Stay hydrated with water or fruit juice.
2. Avoid alcoholic beverages (Sorry, Miss Ruby!).
3. Wear light fabrics and light colors.
4. Wear a lightweight hat in the direct sun.
5. If you must go out in the heat, go out early in the day or in the evening.
6. Avoid rigorous activity in the heat of the day.
7. Stay away from caffeinated beverages.
8. Wear sunscreen.
9. Check any medications you may be on and how they will affect you in direct sun.
10. If you feel dizzy or nauseous, lie down in the shade right away and drink water or fruit juice.

HOW TO WASH AND DRY Tennis Shoes

Remove the loose dirt and mud with a dry scrub brush or by banging the soles of the shoes together a few times.

Use a bucket large enough to hold your shoes. Fill it with warm water and some mild laundry soap.

Take out your shoelaces and let the shoes soak in soapy water for an hour.

Use an old toothbrush and soapy water to scrub the shoes, top and bottom.

Stuff tennis shoes with balled-up newspaper and set them and the shoelaces in the sun to dry.

AUNT IDA'S CHOCOLATE Pecan Pie

3 eggs, slightly beaten

1 cup Karo syrup (light or dark)

1 6-ounce package chocolate chips

1/3 cup sugar

2 Tablespoons melted butter

1 teaspoon vanilla

1 1/2 to 2 cups of pecans, chopped

1 pie crust, unbaked

Sprinkle chocolate chips evenly over unbaked pie crust.

In a large bowl, stir remaining ingredients together and then add pecans.

Pour into pie crust over chocolate chips.

Bake at 350°F for 50 to 60 minutes.

Refrigerate leftovers.

HOW TO GET BLOOD STAINS Out of Clothing

Immediately rinse out the spot with cold water. Simply rubbing the sides of the stain together in the cold water may remove the stain. If it does not come out, then use some bar or liquid hand soap on it.

Peppermint Chocolate Chip Cookies

3/4 cup butter

1/2 cup white sugar

1/2 cup packed brown sugar

1 egg

1 teaspoon vanilla extract

1 teaspoon peppermint extract

1 1/2 cups all-purpose flour

1/4 cup unsweetened cocoa powder

1 teaspoon baking soda

1/4 teaspoon salt

1 cup semisweet chocolate chips

Preheat oven to 350 degrees (F). Grease cookie sheets.

In a large bowl, cream together butter, white sugar and brown sugar until light and fluffy.

Beat in egg, then stir in vanilla and peppermint extracts.

Combine flour, cocoa powder, baking soda and salt; gradually stir into the creamed mixture. Mix in the chocolate chips.

Drop by rounded spoonfuls onto the prepared cookie sheets.

Bake for 12 to 15 minutes.

Recipe for a Hot Toddy

2 lemons

1/4 cup honey

Dash of rum

Squeeze the juice out of the lemons into a saucepan. Use real lemons, not bottled lemon juice.

Add honey and bring to a slow boil.

Let cool for a few minutes and then add a shot of rum. (For a child, simply eliminate the rum.)

Let cool slightly.

This can be taken by teaspoonful or added to a cup of hot tea.

Don't miss out!

Visit the website below and you can sign up to receive emails whenever Teresa Trent publishes a new book. There's no charge and no obligation.

https://books2read.com/r/B-A-FJQD-SFDO

Did you love *A Dash of Murder*? Then you should read *Overdue for Murder*[1] by Teresa Trent!

[2]

Writing Can Be Murder!

Is there life on other planets? Does your love life need a boost? Do you believe in vampires? Don't you wish you were that stylish chick-lit kind of girl? All of these questions seem a little strange, but not if you are attending a book talk...

When local writers present their books at the Pecan Bayou Library, one author gets a killer review. Betsy Livingston, there to talk about her own gripping book on helpful hints around the house, finds herself the prime suspect for the murder. Join

---

1. https://books2read.com/u/mlK1gq

2. https://books2read.com/u/mlK1gq

Betsy in her second mystery as she tries to clear her own name in this hilarious tale of small town Texas life and murder.

Read more at https://teresatrent.com.

Also by Teresa Trent

Pecan Bayou
A Dash of Murder
Overdue for Murder
Doggone Dead
Buzzkill
Burnout
Murder for a Rainy Day
Till Dirt Do Us Part
Oh Holy Fright
Die a Yellow Ribbon

Piney Woods
Murder of a Good Man
A Sneeze to Die For
Die Die Blackbird

Redbird Creek
The Con Man's Daughter

Watch for more at https://teresatrent.com.